"You said…keep it business, and now you're touching me?"

So she did like him. He wanted to see how far this attraction could go. Maybe exact a little revenge for the humiliation she'd put him through when he was in college.

"I just didn't want to come on too strong. I wasn't sure if it was just the idea of the makeover drawing you to me. I wanted to see what happened while I was still me. Before I was your version."

She nodded. "My version?"

"This look seems like it might have been your idea," he said.

She flushed, a pretty blush spreading up her neck and onto her cheeks. "It was. We want to showcase you, Dante."

The way his name sounded on her lips sent a chill down his spine. He wanted her. So any kind of payback was going to be dangerous. He had to remember that.

\* \* \*

*Billionaire Makeover* by Katherine Garbera
is part of The Image Project series.

Dear Reader,

I love a makeover story. What about you? I just like how changing a few things can make me feel like a totally different person. Sometimes the makeover is physical (Dante!) but there is also the more subtle personality makeover (Olive). I drew on a lot of personal experience for both of these characters. This series revolves around makeovers of all types.

Dante, like most of us, really went through it in his twenties finding who he is, and he's happy with what he likes to call his "lumberjack chic" persona. His sexy, deep-timbre voice has listeners clamoring to see the man behind the voice, and no one—not even Dante—thinks he should show up in a flannel shirt and untrimmed beard. So he needs a makeover.

But when a mean girl from his past shows up, Dante is ready to pump the brakes and stick with his flannel. Except Olive has changed since college, or at least gives the impression she has. She knows her stuff too. The only problem is the sparks between the two of them. Dante has the urge to use that attraction to pay her back for humiliating him back in the day.

The more they get to know each other, the harder that plan is to enact, and lots of juicy drama, sex and fun ensue!

I hope you enjoy the launch of The Image Project series.

Happy reading,

*Katherine Garbera*

# KATHERINE GARBERA

———

## BILLIONAIRE MAKEOVER

# DESIRE™

Recycling programs for this product may not exist in your area.

ISBN-13: 978-1-335-58155-6

Billionaire Makeover

Copyright © 2022 by Katherine Garbera

For questions and comments about the quality of this book, please contact us at CustomerService@Harlequin.com.

Harlequin Enterprises ULC
22 Adelaide St. West, 41st Floor
Toronto, Ontario M5H 4E3, Canada
www.Harlequin.com

**Printed in U.S.A.**

**Katherine Garbera** is the *USA TODAY* bestselling author of more than 120 books. She started her career twenty-five years ago at Harlequin Desire writing about strong alpha heroes and feisty heroines and crafting stories that resonate with emotional impact and strong sensuality. She's a Florida girl who has traveled the US, calling different states her home before crossing the pond to settle in the Midlands of the UK, where she lives with her husband and a spoiled miniature dachshund. Find her on the web at www.katherinegarbera.com.

### Books by Katherine Garbera

#### Harlequin Desire

##### *One Night*

*One Night with His Ex*
*One Night, Two Secrets*
*One Night to Risk It All*
*Her One Night Proposal*

##### *Destination Wedding*

*The Wedding Dare*
*The One from the Wedding*
*Secrets of a Wedding Crasher*

##### *The Image Project*

*Billionaire Makeover*

Visit her Author Profile page at Harlequin.com, or katherinegarbera.com, for more titles.

You can also find Katherine Garbera on Facebook, along with other Harlequin Desire authors, at Facebook.com/harlequindesireauthors!

To Josh and Darcey Elser, united in love
and life and one of my favorite couples.
I hope your life together is filled with love,
laughter and happiness.

It's impossible for me to write any book
without the support of my family and friends,
but especially Rob Elser, who made
lockdown a lot of fun. Love you!

# One

Olive Hayes grabbed an iced coffee from Hestia's Hearth bakery and coffee shop in the lobby of her building before meeting her Uber and heading across town to the Inferno Brewing headquarters on North Lake Shore Drive. The company had purchased the old establishment near the Navy Pier and had completely revamped it to house their brewing and bottling facility as well as an office space and a storefront shop. She, like everyone else, had been listening to radio advertisements from the company's CEO, Dante Russo, all winter and spring long, talking about the change of seasons and being authentic.

His message had been received loud and clear

by the public. But Olive thought it was more his dreamy voice, deep and rich in those low, modulated tones, that had somehow reached past advertising and tempted commuters and office workers to stop and fantasize about summer. So she had been pretty excited when the call had come in from Inferno Brewing's marketing manager, Kiki Marin.

The woman had been pretty blunt, saying that Dante needed a full head-to-toe media makeover, and that she'd enlisted their help because of their reputation for being organic with the changes. After the phone call, Olive had immediately taken a look at his social media, which had been quick and easy to do because he had none. Nothing. Not a Facebook or Twitter account. Not even an Instagram or TikTok following. He pretty much, other than showing up on a Reddit board about brewing, had no online presence.

That made her job easier. She was starting with a blank slate as far as everyone was concerned. Though Kiki had mentioned that Dante was a diamond in the rough, she thought the marketing manager must be exaggerating. After all, any man with that voice had to have some game with women— *Hang on! Stop making assumptions*, she scolded herself. Sighing, she sipped her iced coffee and watched the sights of Chicago drift by her window.

Olive had dressed with care for this meeting today. She wore a light purple gingham-print sundress with wide straps, and a pair of wedged heels. And she'd accessorized with a matching purse that her close friend Paisley had made for her last year when she'd been home and had become fixated on sewing. All three of the business partners now had matching bags from her.

She had started her business with Paisley and Delaney right after college. The three of them had been pretty, popular and rich. Also spoiled beyond all good sense, their social media imprint had reflected it. They'd had no choice but to make some changes. At first, they'd started out small. And it had turned out that they'd had a lot of friends who needed the same types of makeovers. Including Delaney's college boyfriend, who got recruited to play professional baseball and needed to make his professional image more "star athlete" and less "drunk frat boy."

That was just one of many transformations they'd made over the last eight years. Her parents didn't understand her business but were proud and supportive of her nonetheless. Her mom had briefly tried to press the fact that she thought Olive should find a husband, but she wasn't ready for that. She had been blunt with her parents and told them she needed to figure out who she was before she attempted to be a part of a couple.

She was still growing and only now starting to really like the woman she was. For many years, she had gone to bed high or drunk and woken up with regrets of her behavior the night before.

She tucked a strand of her reddish-brown hair that had come free from her ponytail behind her ear as the Uber driver pulled to a stop in front of the Inferno Brewing building. Then, pushing her sunglasses up on the top of her head, she smiled at her driver and wished him a nice day before stepping out of the car. Remembering to toss her iced coffee cup in the recycling bin outside the door of the building, she used the selfie camera on her phone to check her lipstick before continuing inside.

Nerves fluttered through her, but she put on her most professional smile as she walked to the security and reception desk to introduce herself.

"I'm Olive Hayes. I have an appointment at ten thirty with Kiki Marin," she said.

"Thank you," the receptionist said as her fingers moved over the keyboard. She nodded and then reached for a guest badge, which she handed to Olive. "Please have a seat. Ms. Marin will be down in a few minutes."

She moved over to the long benches across from the reception desk and took a seat. She opened her bag, pulled out her notebook and made a few notes. Then took a moment to once more review the information that Kiki had sent. They needed Dante made over before the Taste of Chicago festival, which was happening on the Fourth of July weekend. So she had about six weeks to get him in shape. Kiki had mentioned he might need media training and Olive made some notes on that as well. She always asked questions during the first meeting with a client to establish how they handled off-the-cuff answers and how succinct they could be.

After all, no one was interested in listening to anyone ramble on about their product.

"Hi there, Olive. I'm Kiki Marin. So nice to meet you," the young woman said, holding her hand out.

Olive smiled and shook it while standing. "The pleasure is all mine. I have to admit I'm intrigued to meet the man behind the Inferno Brewing ads. Like everyone else who has heard him on the radio, I'm excited to see what he looks like."

Kiki snorted. "Once you do, promise you won't run for the hills."

"I'm sure that won't be an issue," she said. All the while wondering what exactly she was going to encounter when they walked into Dante Russo's office.

Kiki led the way down a traditional workplace hallway. And stepped into the open doorway.

"Ready for us, Dante?"

"I am," he said in that deep timbre that Olive had already come to love. She peaked past the corner but stopped short as she took in a massive amount of curly hair around a face that was hard to discern behind the thick, unruly beard. And when he stood up, she noticed he had on a gray loose-fitting T-shirt, a denim long-sleeved shirt over it, and a pair of khaki cargo pants.

She finally got what Kiki meant. This was going to be a big challenge.

*Olive Hayes was here.*

It was almost hard to believe that the girl he'd had a massive crush on in college, the girl who'd rejected him with a mean cut-down and forced him to make some tough life decisions, was here. In the flesh.

Standing in his doorway…looking more breath-taking than ever.

He glanced at Kiki, who raised both eyebrows at him in that warning way of hers. Telling him to be cool and play nice.

"Hello. I'm Dante Russo," he said, walking over to her. But his civility was just a pretense. In fact, he was now more determined than ever to *not* change his image because she was the woman Kiki had hired. He didn't think he could work with her, but he would give her a chance because Kiki thought she was the best person for the job.

"It's so wonderful to meet you," she gushed. "Of course, I recognize your voice and already half love you. It's fabulous!"

He realized that she didn't recognize him from college. But why would she? He'd been slightly tubby, thanks to years of eating his mom's home cooking and not really exercising. And he'd been Danny back then. No facial hair, just his out-of-control curly hair. Good. He could deal with her not remembering him.

"Thanks."

"You can totally see why we need you," Kiki added. "I mean, that voice is great but…"

He shot his marketing manager a sharp look. Kiki was pushing it this morning.

"But *what*?" Olive said. "What I see is everything I expected from the voice behind Inferno Brewing. A man who is authentic and not about artifice. I can see that you might want a little polish if you're going to do print and video ads, but the truth is, I think you're going to want to stay true to who you are. If we send in some Hollywood-looking hunk, your followers will see through it."

He looked over at Olive again, seeing past the college girl to the professional woman standing in his office. Her shoulder-length red hair was smooth and pulled back in a low ponytail. She had an easy smile on her lovely heart-shaped face, but he had a hard time getting past her mouth. He'd spent hours in college watching her mouth while she'd been talking, and fantasizing about it. Mean girl she might have been, but she had the kind of smile that made a man feel like he was a giant, and her mouth with the cute cupid's bow on the top and full bottom lip always made him want to kiss her.

She got it. He wasn't sure if she was saying he'd never be a Hollywood hunk, which he didn't fault her with, but he was pretty sure she was saying she'd work with him and not try to make him into something he wasn't.

"I agree," Kiki said. "I'm sorry if I was coming on too strong, Dante. I just want this new launch and your reveal to be flawless."

"I get it. I do. No offense taken," he said. And there wasn't. He had no delusions about the man he was. In part, thanks to Olive, who made him take stock in who he was and stop trying to be something and someone he wasn't. "So where do we start? Also, can I offer you a drink?"

"I'd love a water," she murmured. "Let's set up your parameters. Once I know what you want to do, we can get to work creating the man who will match the fantasy that your voice has conjured."

She took a seat at the small round table he had in the corner of his office; Kiki joined her while he grabbed drinks for them.

The next hour was just chatting about the launch Kiki had planned for the company, including a big VIP red-carpet event they were hosting during Taste of Chicago. He had a few smaller shindigs leading up to the July event, but before all that took place, Kiki wanted to relaunch their social media platforms with him as the face of Inferno Brewing. Not just the voice.

A short while later, his employee left for an appointment and he and Olive were alone. She looked up from her notes.

"That's what *Kiki* needs from you, but you're the person who has to make all these changes. What are your no-goes?"

"No-goes?"

"Things you absolutely won't do," she said. "Like hair, beard, clothing… I think we are going to have to try to find some new outfits that fit your outdoorsy, laid-back vibe but aren't…"

"Lumberjack chic?"

She laughed and nodded at him. When she did, her hair moved and the scent of strawberries drifted toward him. He smiled back.

"Yeah. So…"

"I don't mind a haircut or beard trim. Someone once said I had a weak chin, so I think I'll keep the beard if you don't mind," he said.

"Who said that?" she asked. "People can be so thoughtless with their comments. I'm sure you have a great chin, but we can work with the beard."

*She'd* said it. It had been one of many things that she'd listed as a reason why she'd never go out with him, much less dance with him at a frat party. "A woman I once knew."

"She was probably just full of herself and trying to be all that… I've got a guy who I use for hair and beards, so I'll make you an appointment with him. Do you have time today? I think the sooner we get moving, the better. We have six weeks until the last event, but your first one is…" She looked down at her notes.

He tuned out, thinking about what she had said about the girl… Had she been full of herself back then? He knew *he* had, and after the public rejection, had realized that he hadn't really known Olive at all, had just seen a pretty girl and started crushing on her like he'd done so many times in the past, but as they'd worked together on a group project, it had changed from passing fancy into something more for him.

But he'd never made that mistake again.

"Does that work?" she asked, breaking into his thoughts.

"I'm sorry, I missed that," he said gruffly.

She put her hand over his and an electric tingle went through him. She immediately pulled her hand back and licked her lips. "I asked if you could do a hair appointment this afternoon?"

He agreed and she gathered her things and left a few minutes later. Dante walked to the window in his office, watching the plaza until she'd exited, before realizing what he was doing. He couldn't deny how gorgeous and sexy she was. But no matter what, he wasn't going to fall for Olive Hayes again. He was too smart, successful and self-assured for that.

# Two

Olive used the Slack chat to update Paisley and Delaney about their new client. Mainly as a distraction from Dante. She hadn't expected the "lumberjack chic" guy to be so…*hot*. There was an understated sexiness about him that she couldn't deny. And she wasn't about to allow herself to have the hots for a client. So she allowed herself a brief thought of the keen intelligence in his green eyes and how she'd caught him looking at her in a distinctly unprofessional but man-woman-I-like-you way, and then got busy.

She had already arranged for Pietro, her hair guy, to be at the Inferno Brewing offices that afternoon to try to tame that crazy mane and beard Dante had going on.

She also needed to do some shopping for a new wardrobe for him, but truly, she had no idea where to start.

Olive knew she needed his measurements, of course, and would probably do some custom suits for his big red-carpet events, but honestly, that guy needed help ASAP, so she'd do some off-the-rack shopping.

She picked up her phone and shot him a text.

Hey, it's Olive Hayes. I need your sizes to get some clothing options.

Uh, like what? I have some nice jeans and khakis at home.

Rolling her eyes, she called him instead of texting back.

He answered on the first ring, that deep rumble once again messing with the image of the real man. "Hey, I'm not being difficult, but I hate to waste money on clothing."

His voice sent a warm shiver through her. Olive shook her head, forcing her thoughts back to work. She'd already guessed he didn't spend a lot on his clothes. "I get it. But we need to have an idea of what your image will be. I just want to get some different options pulled together so once your hair and beard are done, we can move forward. If you want, I can go through your actual wardrobe and pull some things."

He sighed. "I don't have time to do that this morning."

"That makes sense. Just give me some sizes and I'll pull clothes from the shops I have accounts with until we are sure that you like it."

"Fine. I guess if I agreed to listen to your advice, I shouldn't be fighting you every step of the way," he grumbled.

"Well, it would make things easier if you didn't. But I totally get where you are coming from, Dante. I mean, you're selling your beer, not yourself, and I do understand that. The only thing is…your voice has made people think they know you, and I think your marketing manager is totally right to capitalize on it. So I'll do my best to keep her happy and not be too intrusive on you."

"I appreciate it. I've authorized you on my Black Amex," he said. "I'll send you the number so you can use it to make your purchases."

"You don't have to—"

"I do. If I'm doing this, I want to do it right. Also, while you are shopping for me, I need a new suit to do this stuff Kiki wants me to."

"I'll have a tailor come and take your measurements for that," she told him.

"Great," he said. "I've got to go to a meeting. But where do I need to be for the makeover?"

His voice was already conjuring up the image of him after the conversion and, for a moment, she thought she'd like to see him at her place for the makeover. She wanted to see what he looked like all trimmed up. That voice was promising a man who would rock her world. Dang, what was going on with her today? Why was Dante Russo stirring these kinds of thoughts?

"Kiki offered your conference room. I'll have some clothes and stuff for you to try after your haircut and style."

"Ugh. You know this sounds like those makeover shows my mom watches," he said.

"It is exactly like that," she replied. She, for one, couldn't wait to see him transformed. Would he be as sexy as she was imagining? "It'll be fun."

"Yeah, right," he said. "See ya later, Olive."

"Later, Dante."

After he hung up, she got a number of texts, including one from American Express authorizing her on Dante's card. He also sent her his sizes, which were smaller than she thought they'd be. But the clothing he'd worn in the meeting this morning had been sort of baggy. She took him at his word and started shopping.

Olive had always loved shopping, and this was one part of her job she really enjoyed. Instead of shopping for the man she'd met that morning, she kept the image his voice had evoked in her head, the one with the whiskey-rough rasp that had been the soundtrack to her fantasies lately. She bought clothes that were fitting with that man.

"Hiya," Delaney said as she linked her arm through Olive's at the fragrance counter in Bloomingdale's.

She wasn't surprised to see her friend and business partner. They all had that friend tracker on their phones and she knew Delaney didn't have any clients at the moment. Her friend had shoulder-length blond hair with darker roots. As heir to the Alexander dish soap fortune, the media portrayed her as preferring her jet-setting life to working, but Delaney was grounded and worked just as hard as Olive and Paisley. She made sure to be caught by the paparazzi with her society boyfriends late at night but then always showed up to work the next morning.

"Hey. What do you think of this?" she asked, holding up a fragrance card for Delaney to sniff.

"Who's it for?"

"Inferno Brewing," she said.

"I like it, but what about this one?" her friend asked, reaching for another fragrance that had a deeper woodsy tone.

Olive closed her eyes and thought of Dante for the first time. Remembering that spark when she'd touched his hand. Realizing that she had been turned on by him… It had to have been his voice.

"I love it. Perfect." She purchased the cologne, aftershave and body wash and had it sent to Inferno Brewing's offices. "What's up?"

"I think that Malcolm is seeing someone else," Delaney said as they walked out of the store onto Chicago's magnificent mile.

"*What?* I thought he loved you," Olive said, not really shocked. Delaney had a history of dating men who were users. For some reason, her friend was drawn to men who lied. She'd never had a healthy relationship and Olive wished there was something she could do or say to help Delaney with that. But she didn't really know how to help.

"So he said, though I'm beginning to think he just told me that to get invited to Dad's New Year's Eve bash. You know how stingy he is with the invites, and Malcolm definitely doesn't have anything that Dad wants."

"Except your love," Olive said.

Delaney snorted, and Olive hugged her friend. "I'm sorry."

"Me too. But it's okay. Do you have time for lunch?"

Olive glanced at her watch. "I can do a quick one. I have to be back at Inferno by two."

Olive's humiliating rejection of him as a college junior had been life changing. He'd made up his mind to stop trying to be anything other than himself. But he'd also decided to stop lying. Not that he'd been conning everyone he met, but he had spent a lot of time deluding himself about the man he was. After Olive, he'd stopped trying so hard to force himself to be someone he wasn't. So, as he waited for her hair and beard guy to show up, he debated if he should just tell her who he was.

Would his name even matter to her? Would she even remember?

And was this about him or her? He blew out a breath. Was there any advantage to telling Olive that she'd said rude things to him in college? His dad, a science fiction writer, always said "do no harm." The man liked to talk about life in credos like that. Yet the older Dante got, the more sense it made.

Telling Olive might give him a bit of an edge over her. But in no way would it be helpful to their working relationship. He had no time to ponder that, however, because Kiki burst into his office without knocking, as she was prone to do when she was excited about something.

"Boss! We just got a request to sponsor the main tent at Milwaukee's beer fest in a few weeks. I was tempted to turn them down after they were so jerky to us five years ago—"

"But we are bigger than that kind of pettiness," he deadpanned.

"Yeah, and it will be perfect to introduce the world to the hottie CEO whose voice they've already fallen in love with."

His jaw twitched. "I don't know about the *hottie CEO* bit, but yes, it will be nice to have my new image and all that. Do they have a music act for the tent yet?"

"Affirmative! And it's your favorite, After Dark. I mean, it's pretty much like fate wants us to do this," Kiki said.

"Fate seems to be very busy today," he mused. That might explain Olive Hayes walking back into his life.

His marketing manager quirked her brow. "What have I missed?"

"Nothing," he said, not about to discuss anything pre-Dante's Inferno with Kiki. She was a great person but also worked for him, and he didn't want to talk about those years. *Ever.* "Just the band, the timing and the festival. I think that the hair person is supposed to be here soon, will you check on that?"

"Sure thing, boss. Everything's coming up Inferno!" she said in a singsong way as she left his office.

He'd needed someone with her cheery optimism when he'd started marketing the beer, and Kiki was still a gem. He walked over to his desk to pick up his phone and noticed that Olive had sent him several images of clothing options via text.

Dante wasn't sure about any of them, but Kiki was right, he wasn't a microbrewer anymore and it was time to look the part. He'd moved out of his tiny flat into a large mansion when he'd made his first million. Despite his current look, for a while he'd hit the club scene and been wearing trendy clothes and making sure he looked the part as he dated his way through the well-heeled society, but that had soured quickly.

Money might have made him more desirable to the Olive Hayeses of the world, but it hadn't felt satisfying to Dante. He'd kept sleeping with women, trying to get some kind of revenge against Olive, but it hadn't taken him long to realize that he wasn't moving forward. So he'd dropped out of the dating scene for a few years to try and find himself. The radio ads that everyone had fallen for had started out as reflections he'd been having on his morning runs. Words that had pulled him out of the dark place he'd started heading toward when he'd gotten what he thought he'd wanted and found it to be hollow.

There was a rap on the door frame and he glanced up.

"Dante? Kiki told me you were expecting me," a man said.

He turned to face him. "Yes. You are?"

"Pietro Savarino. I can see we have a lot to work with," he said. "Do you have an idea of what you want?"

"I think I'm supposed to just put myself in your hands," he replied. "But I would like to keep some of my facial hair."

"Not a problem. Let's get started."

Pietro was as friendly as most hairdressers were. It had been a long time since Dante had cut his hair—

not since his party days. So he was surprised when Pietro finished and he looked at himself in the mirror. Not bad. Pietro had kept the length on the top of his head, which allowed his curls to just look thick instead of untamed. The beard trim defined his jawline and gave him a serious air.

He walked out of the bathroom. "I like it. Thanks."

"You're welcome," Pietro said.

"Wow," Olive said, striding into his office. "We might not need to worry about your wardrobe, Dante."

Their eyes met and he felt something go through him, something electric and sexual. *Something that wasn't happening*, he told his body firmly. He wasn't going to fall into the Olive spell again. This time he was old enough and wise enough to know better. But seeing her reaction…it did make him wonder if his revenge with society babes hadn't worked because it hadn't been with her.

Dante could still remember the first time he'd met Olive. They'd had a psych class together and had been assigned the same group. She'd smiled at everyone and kind of taken the leadership role. Looking back, he realized he'd been fooled by her easy smile. Dante had always been smart and Olive had used that to her advantage, bringing him coffees when they met and thanking him for doing her part of the project.

He'd been so smitten with her smiles and the coffees, it hadn't occurred to him that she was just being nice to him so he'd do the bulk of the work. After that semester…he'd made her into his fantasy woman. And their interactions from his point of view had always seemed like she felt the same way about him. In retrospect, he suspected she had only been kind to him when she'd needed him to pick up the slack on a group project or to donate to her sorority charity.

After his humiliation at her hands, he'd vowed to never be anyone's pawn again. He'd turned into the male version of Olive for a while, using women and breaking hearts. Something he hadn't liked in himself. But this was Olive…

What if he let this thing between them develop? What if he let her fall for him and then did to her what she'd done to him? What if he finally got closure with her?

But he'd have to be more like her and the woman she'd been than the man he had built himself into, and he wasn't sure if that was a bad thing or not.

Olive couldn't believe the difference in Dante. Just a haircut and beard trim, and everything that she'd felt from that tingle when their hands brushed was confirmed. Of course, she knew that reaction was shallow and one of the things she'd been trying to change about herself over the last eight years.

Yet if she was being totally honest with herself, she'd been attracted to him even before the haircut. He'd been a bit shaggy, but he'd also been nice and direct, and they'd had that combustible moment. But she knew herself. She tended to build men into what she wanted them to be.

"Let's go and look at the clothes I selected. Kiki caught me up on the beer fest, which will be great for a first outing. I think we can look at getting you some media training before that. Though you might not need it," she said as they left his office, and he followed her down the hall to the conference room where she'd set up the wardrobe options.

Olive squared her shoulders. She'd just be professional and totally ignore the fact that he'd turned into the hot fantasy man she'd imagined when she'd first heard his voice on the radio. She could do that. But that didn't stop her from thinking about how much she'd like to kiss him. Just put her hands on that masculine jaw of his with the neatly trimmed beard to see if there was any truth to what her hormones were telling her.

"I'd like that," he said.

Startled, she stopped to look over her shoulder at him. He put his hand out to steady her as he'd been closer than she'd expected and had stumbled.

"What?"

"The media training," he clarified. "I'd like that. I do okay when we record for the marketing campaign, but that's scripted. I'm not sure what to say when it's more informal."

She was pretty sure he was just saying that. There

was nothing about Dante Russo that wasn't confident. Even with his long hair and beard, he'd exuded a sense of strength and authority that had made her notice him.

"You'll do great," she said, trying not to keep staring at him, though it was hard to look away. She'd thought that he'd be hot just from the image in her head, but this was something else. Almost as if Dante had become that faceless man she'd always dreamed of meeting. He was the embodiment of everything she'd always wanted to find in a man.

"Was there something else? You stopped so quickly before, like you'd forgotten something," he said.

She blushed then tried to cover it by looking away. "Not really. I was just making sure you were still behind me."

He arched one eyebrow at her but didn't comment further. "Of course. So what should I expect in here?"

She nodded and cleared her throat. "I have styled some mannequins so we can get an idea of what you like and would feel comfortable in. I mean, there is a black-tie ensemble that you're going to need, but the other stuff for your festivals and everyday appearances will be more up to you."

"Black tie?"

"You said VIP event. I think you want to go in there looking like you belong there, and women will die when they see you in a tux," she said.

"They'll *die*?" he teased.

She smiled at that. Was it her imagination or was he being flirty? "Yes. Probably men too. Everyone loves a sharp-dressed man."

"ZZ Top?"

"I'm originally from Texas," she said as if that explained why she loved the band. But the truth was that her mama had loved it and she'd grown up with them. "You?"

He winked. "Northwesterner through and through. But I'm told I have great taste in music."

So he *was* flirting with her. Olive could see it in his eyes, and she couldn't resist him. She wanted to flirt back but then, as soon as that debutante training kicked in, she shook her head and turned to start walking again.

That woman wasn't who she wanted to be. No matter that this thing with Dante hadn't felt calculated or like she was trying to lure him in to find a wealthy husband—which had been her main goal until college. Finding herself had revealed that she'd relied too heavily on those old behaviors when she wasn't sure of herself. And she needed to be her most confident to meet Dante's fire with her own.

That meant not flirting with him just because he was handsome and she loved his voice. She deserved better from herself…and so did he.

"So this is it," she said. "These mannequins are

the casual everyday looks I thought might work best for you."

She'd also brought along Sam and Ted, who had worked in the fashion industry before coming to work for her. "Just look over the outfits and pick the one that sort of suits your style."

He put his hand on her shoulder and she looked up at him. "Yes?"

"Sorry if I crossed a line out there," he said. "It's been a while since I've left the brewery."

She licked her suddenly dry lips and turned closer to him so that her colleagues wouldn't overhear. "You didn't. I like you, Dante, but you're a client, so I think maybe just keeping it professional would be best."

"Agreed." He dropped his hand and moved past her.

Releasing a quavering breath, she stood there, watching him talk and joke with Sam and Ted. They were switching some things on the mannequins, but she was hardly paying attention. Had *she* been the one to cross a line? Maybe she shouldn't have said anything, but the truth was, she did like him, and that warning had been more for herself than for him.

This feeling in the pit of her stomach was one she hadn't had in years. The last time she'd felt this way, her entire world had crashed around her. She'd been called out for being a mean girl by some of her sorority sisters, and she wasn't sure that she was ready for that again. She'd risen out of the ashes and rebuilt her life, but the truth was that she was still finding her way back and trying to be the woman she'd always wanted to be.

For a reformed mean girl, that wasn't always easy. And seeing Dante's ease with everyone reminded her of the woman she wanted to be. She was determined to ensure that she was.

Professional. She could do that.

# Three

The more he caught glimpses of himself in the mirror, the more he felt himself slipping back into the arrogant guy he used to be. He tried to fight it, but he presumed the look had been inspired by some guy in *GQ* who was a designer for Givenchy. Dante didn't follow the big fashion houses but he liked the black patterned trousers, black boots and T-shirt look.

"I'll try that one first."

"Great," Sam said. "I'll get everything set up in the changing area while Ted takes you through the rest of the outfits."

He watched as Olive went to the screen that had been set up in the corner of his conference room.

He had to admit he was surprised to see how they'd changed a room normally used for meetings with his team and investors into a dressing room and display area for the outfits.

He ignored Olive as best as he could, trying to focus on Ted, who was describing another outfit they thought would work for the beer fest. But the truth was, he was very aware of her. Aware of the feelings she stirred in him. It wasn't the lust that bothered him. She'd always been hot, so being attracted to her wasn't exactly a shock.

It was the anger.

He'd been telling himself for years that he'd found a sort of Zen-type bliss toward his past and the path he was on. But one touch, one proffered kiss, and he was back to the asshole he'd become when he'd made his first million and, fuck him, also that earnest college kid who'd asked her out. Who'd believed all the bull that his parents had fed him growing up about being himself and that everyone he met would see the truth of the person he was.

"Sure. You know what? I'll try on everything you guys have for me. Just get it prepped. Am I doing a movie-style montage try-on?" he asked. "I'll blast some tunes to set the mood."

Ted threw his head back and laughed. "Only if you want to. Just think of it as…well, I don't know what would make sense to you…maybe a beer flight before you commit to buying a case?"

"Got it," he said. "That works."

"What works?" Olive asked as she pocketed her phone and rejoined them.

He noticed that she kept her distance and, if he was honest, her smile didn't quite reach her eyes now. Had he done that?

Dante clenched his jaw. He didn't want to give her any real emotions. He wanted her to be his cruel ice queen who just moved through life not realizing that she was leaving a wake of roadkill behind her. But there was definitely something there that he hadn't noticed earlier.

He wondered if he could coax that smile back up to her eyes. Was he really doing this?

Yes, he was. He wanted to see if Olive had changed at all. It had been ten years since he'd seen her, so he suspected she had, but had she just become more aloof or was this something else?

"I told them to just set up everything for me and I'd try it all on. I mean, looking at the outfits doesn't really help me."

"Why not?"

"I'm not visual," he said, turning and leaning in to test a theory. "I'm much more tactile."

He lifted his hand, tucking a strand of hair that had fallen forward behind her ear. Olive's breath caught and her lips parted as she looked up at him. The moment their eyes met, something shifted between them, and he saw that there *was* some real emotion in the beautiful brown depths. But he didn't have time to contemplate what that meant—for either of them—because her brow furrowed and she took his hand, drawing him across the room.

"Is something wrong?"

"Yes!" she huffed out. "What's up with you? We agreed in the hallway to keep it business and now you're touching me?"

So she *did* like him. What was he going to do with that? He caught a glimpse of himself with his haircut and his beard trim—he looked the part of the billionaire brewer and he didn't hesitate to let that flow through him. He wanted to see how far this attraction could go. Maybe exact a little revenge for the humiliation she'd put him through when he was in college.

Was it fair?

Hell.

Probably not. But in the words of Olive Hayes, "Who said life was fair?"

"I just didn't want to come on too strong. I wasn't sure if it was just the idea of the makeover drawing you to me. I wanted to see what happened while I was still me. Before I was your version."

She swallowed. "My version?"

"The Givenchy look seems like it might have been your idea," he said.

She flushed, an adorable blush spreading up her neck and onto her cheeks. "It was. But I pretty much directed all of the outfits. Sam is good at pulling together accessories, and Ted excels at taking my ideas and making them unique so you don't look like everyone else. We want to showcase you, Dante."

The way his name sounded on her lips sent a chill down his spine and made his cock harden. He shifted his stance and nodded. He wanted her, so any kind of revenge was going to be dangerous. Best he remember that.

This woman had hurt him once before, and if he started down this path, it was going to be with the knowledge that he had to do so with a modicum of caution. This was his con, his game, *not hers*, and if he played it right, he'd leave Olive feeling just as he had all those years ago.

He wasn't at all proud that he wanted to hurt her the way she had hurt him, but there was no arguing with this part of himself. After all, she'd shaken him from his comfy world as a little princeling where he had been popular in his friend group and hadn't realized he was a tubby nerd. It was only her comment that had made him take a hard look at the man he was and what the outside world saw. She'd shaken his belief in who he was and it had started him on a path toward becoming what other people valued… or specifically, what Olive valued. A buff guy with attitude. A sort of alpha asshole.

It had taken him years to come back to himself. Making beer had given him that path between the boy he'd been in college and the man he was today.

He'd been arrogant, he realized, in thinking all of those emotions were in the past. Because there was a part of him that wanted to hurt her. And as much as he didn't like that about himself, he couldn't really change it either.

"Thank you, Olive. I look forward to being show-cased," he said.

Sam called him over and he walked away from her, very aware that she watched him as he did so. All of a sudden some of his trepidation at this idea to exact some sweet retribution slid away. Hopefully, if he kept things light, he would walk away unscathed.

Olive and her staff stood off to the side while Dante was in the changing area. She kept a nice stream of small talk going with them. Olive genuinely liked Sam and Ted. They had been with her from the beginning when she and her friends had started IDG Brand Imaging. They knew the new Olive the best, she thought. But at the same time she worried about something that Dante had said.

He'd played into her secret fears that she was only attracted to him because she was making him into her vision of the man his voice evoked.

Was there any way to be sure she wasn't?

She doubted it. She'd picked out clothes for Dante that were both edgy and on trend without appearing like he'd stopped by the mall on his way to an event. She wanted to see him all dressed up like the men she dated and rule out that there was any part of her that was attracted to him because of the makeover.

But if her past had taught her anything, it was that no matter what she tried, she always made dangerous choices when it came to who she was attracted to. She wanted to be like Paisley, who could be so chill about the men she dated, knowing her fortune was part of why they were knocking on her door, but Olive had never been able to do that.

She had always been looking for a guy she could picture right next to her in her perfect life.

It didn't matter that she'd already decided a perfect preplanned future wasn't one she wanted; inevitably she was always drawn to the men who would have fit that plan. She sighed.

"What is it?" Sam asked. "Are you worried about the outfits?"

She smiled and shook her head. "I have a feeling we could leave Dante in his button-down flannel and khakis and he'd still kill it."

"Me too," Ted said. "That man has the carriage to pull off anything."

"Agreed."

"Are you guys talking about me?" Dante asked as he stepped from behind the screen.

"Damn."

"Oh, yeah."

Olive ignored her team and walked over to him, trying to be professional. But how was that even going to be possible? The dark T-shirt he'd put on brought out the warm tones of his tanned skin and the color of his eyes that, she noticed for the first time, were more gray than green. Once their gazes met, she couldn't look away. He'd added the thick gold chain the mannequin had been wearing, but on Dante it was too much. He didn't need anything to draw the eye.

With the boots, he towered over her. The pants were a little loose but once they measured him, they'd have them fitted. She walked around him, on the pretense of checking out the entire look, but the truth was she needed to take a few steadying breaths.

How had Dante been hiding this lean, hot bod beneath his clothes? Or even more importantly, why had he?

"So...?"

He turned to face her, his broad shoulders blocking out the rest of the room, and she put her hand on her throat and shrugged. "It's great. Do you like it?"

"Actually, I do. When I saw this dumb zipper on my thigh... I'm not going to lie, I rolled my eyes, but with the outfit, it works."

"It does. I mean, I don't know if you want this to be an everyday look, but it works on you. We'll need to take your measurements and then I'll send everything you are keeping to the tailor."

He turned toward the three mirrors they had set up off to the side and walked over to look at himself.

He took out his cell phone, snapped a photo, and then he sent it to someone.

"I need to get Kiki's approval. Since this is her idea," Dante said.

Kiki. His cute little marketing manager. Was there more between the two of them?

"Why isn't she here?"

"She's running a focus group," he replied, then chuckled at his phone. "This outfit works."

*Glad the marketing girl approved it*, she thought sarcastically. Then checked herself. That was mean. And she liked Kiki.

"Good. On to the next one."

Olive took a step back and walked to one of the windows at the other end of the room. Jeez. What was going on with her today?

She hadn't been that off-the-cuff catty in a long time. Had she just been fooling herself thinking she'd been making progress? Was she still just a mean girl behind a pretty smile? She hoped not. But her thoughts toward Kiki made her question her supposed growth.

She probably needed to take a break. "Sam, I've got to take a call real quick. Can you handle this?"

"Sure. Ted and I've got this."

Olive walked away faster than she wanted to, stopping to pick up her matching purse and catching a glimpse of herself in the mirror on the way out. Still dressed on trend, like she always was. Lately she'd been smiling at herself in the mirror, but the expression on her face was one she knew too well. One that the paparazzi called her Bitch Babe look. One that she'd hoped she'd seen the last of.

As soon as she was in the hallway, she hurried to the ladies' room down the hall. Closing the door behind her and locking it, she shook her head. All this time she'd thought the good deeds she'd been doing, helping people correct the things that were holding them back, was earning her some sort of karmic black ink, but she realized that her ledger was still full of red.

That had been a wake-up call she'd needed to keep working on herself. This wasn't her time to stop.

Dante tried on the rest of the outfits, disappointed that Olive wasn't in the room, though maybe that was for the best. He put his regular clothes back on, but now they didn't feel right. Didn't jibe with the image in his mind of who he was.

Or, more precisely, the man who he *wanted* to be. He'd worked hard to reinvent himself—but seeing Olive again had messed with his head. Potentially setting him on a path that he really didn't want to be on. He winced. Contemplating some kind of sexual revenge against Olive was seriously messed up. But he couldn't think about that right now. He needed to take a breather, and had the perfect partner in crime in mind.

He pulled his phone out and texted his best friend and former college roommate, Max Richardson.

I need to get out on the water. Drinks and sails tonight at 7?

Dude, yes. Have to confirm with Mia.

Mia was Max's wife. They'd always sort of been couple goals for him, and Dante realized he needed to reinforce his better instincts. Max always grounded him and brought him back to himself.

About five minutes later his phone pinged.

Mia said yes.

Dante chuckled and sent back the thumbs-up. Then pocketing his phone, he walked out from behind the screens in his conference room. He was surprised to see Olive was back.

He could tell she'd returned in "business mode." She'd put on a double-breasted navy jacket over the outfit she'd been wearing. Only problem was, the jacket hugged her figure, and the harder she tried to erect the "work" barrier between them, the more he saw it as a challenge.

And he'd never been able to resist… He wanted to believe it was a challenge he couldn't resist. His gut said it was Olive.

"I didn't want to interrupt you, but we need to get your measurements to send with the clothes. Sam and Ted have gone, do you mind if I take them?" she asked.

"I don't think so," he said. He'd never been measured for clothes. Even for Max's wedding, when he'd been the best man, because it had been a beach wedding so no tux fittings had been necessary.

"Great. This will be quick and painless," she promised. "Sorry I missed seeing the rest of your try-ons, but I heard you liked most of the stuff we picked out."

"I did," he admitted. "Sam said you'd send over some wardrobe suggestions and I would order them."

"Yes," Olive said, taking a tape measure from her bag, along with a notebook. She set it on the table that had been pushed to the side. "Will that work?"

"Sure. Or you can just order what you like from the stuff I choose. I don't need to be involved in that," he said.

"Fine," she murmured. "I'll do your shoulders and chest measurements first."

She moved in closer, and he closed his eyes. She smelled like summer. The scent of sun-filled days and flowers on the breeze assaulted his senses. Immediately, he opened his eyes and saw that she was staring at his chest.

She was so close that they were almost touching. And a moment later, as he shifted his weight from one foot to the other…he *did* make contact. Even if it was just his arm brushing against the skirt of her sundress. Still, he heard that intake of her breath and realized she was as affected by their nearness as he was. He stepped back. "Arms out or at my sides?" he asked. The sooner she got done measuring him, the better it would be for both of them.

She directed him and took all of his measurements, save for his inseam, which he just rattled off before she attempted to get that too. He didn't trust himself if she touched his thighs. He was on the edge, closer to it than he'd been since his string of one-night stands almost five years ago.

"That should do it," she said. "Listen, I heard what you said earlier, and I want you to know that I am not trying to make you into my version of who you are."

"You're not?" he asked, leaning against the table and crossing his ankles, going for a relaxed but interested pose so maybe his hormones would calm down.

"No. When you hired me, it was to help you brand the image of the man your customers see when they hear you on the radio. I know that we aren't going to meet everyone's expectations, but I think with these outfits and the haircut, you are going to see *yourself* in the mirror, not anyone else's version of you. And if you don't, let me know, and we can go back and find something else that's more comfortable for you."

He thought about what she was saying. The amount of time and effort she'd already put into this makeover was a lot. Sure, she'd just been on the clock one day, but she'd gotten her people out here at no small cost. And, though he felt a little bit out of his comfort zone with all this attention on him, he actually liked the wardrobe selections she and her team had chosen for him.

"I'm good. I didn't mean what I said as an insult earlier."

"I didn't take it as one," she returned, putting her stuff in her bag. "I just know that I can come off as sort of pushy when it comes to this part of the image rebrand."

"You can? I hadn't noticed."

"Liar. Tomorrow, I have some media training folks to consult with you. Also, Kiki wants you to do some videos. I'm not sure where."

"She wants us to be in a field of hops."

She widened her eyes. "Oh, is there one around here?"

"No. We get them from a farm in Oregon, but we can improvise. Just something outdoors."

She frowned and sort of grimaced.

"What is it?"

"Outdoors is harder to shoot. The lighting can't be controlled, and sound can be hard… But if that's what you want, we will make it work."

She wasn't backing down or insisting that things just go her way. This was new, and he realized before he pushed forward with his make-her-fall-for-him-then-dump-her plan, he should try to get to know this new woman. "Let's brainstorm. I'll have Kiki email you and we can talk logistics and what makes the most sense."

"That works for me," she said, starting toward the door.

He followed her out and escorted her to the elevators at the end of the hall. "Thanks for everything today, Olive. I really didn't know if this was going to work, but I like it. Don't tell Kiki, she'll never let me live it down."

"My lips are sealed," she murmured, drawing her fingers over her lips.

He stared at her mouth and groaned as he realized he wanted to kiss her. He started to lean in closer. Her hand came to his chest, but not to push him away, he realized as her fingers knotted the fabric of his shirt.

But then the elevator door opened behind her and he had no choice but to step back. She licked her lips and nodded at him before getting into the elevator.

# Four

Olive needed a drink. And it was Thursday, so that meant margaritas with her girls. She took an Uber to the rooftop bar where they always met and was surprised to see Paisley and her new guy waiting in the corner booth. Normally this was girls' night and Olive really needed to let loose with all of the dirty truth she'd realized about herself today.

She felt that inner bitchiness stirring and that just ticked her off. After years of owning it and not being mean, she was struggling today. She forced a smile and was determined to be the kindest, most sweet part of her personality even when she saw that Paisley had brought her boyfriend.

"Hey, you two," she said. Realizing she didn't remember Paisley's boyfriend's name.

"Hello yourself. Olive, this is Jack. Not sure you remember meeting him at Hestia's Hearth the other day."

"I do remember," she said with the million-watt smile that had helped her win Miss Texas back in the day. "It's so nice to see you again. What are you two drinking? I'll grab you refills when I go get mine."

"Margs of course," Paisley said.

"Be right back," she told them, taking her credit card from her wallet and leaving her bag at the table.

She waded through the line to get to the bar and figured since no one could see her she could have a little sulk. She was going to allow herself to be pouty about not having girls' night until she ordered the drinks, and then she was going to let it go.

Someone put an arm around her waist and rested their head against her shoulder. *Delaney.* She looked as sad as she had seemed earlier when they were shopping. Olive hugged her back. "More bad news?"

"Yeah. Malcolm apparently *is* dumping me. He kicked me out of his home. Can you believe that? I mean, I pulled up and my bags were all sitting in front of the house. Lyle wasn't happy at trying to get all those things into the car."

"Why was your driver with you?" she asked.

"I was going to drink my way through Malcolm's cellar as payback," Delaney said. "Anyway, I texted Dad's housekeeper and she let me into his house.

Ugh, I can't believe I have to find another place. I sublet my place when I moved in with Malcolm."

"You could stay with me if you want," Olive said. "I have a guest room and I'd love the company."

"If you won't mind, then I'd love it." Delaney shuddered. "I can't bear to live with Dad. It's almost as bad as Malcolm trying to humiliate me."

"I'm not sure what Malcolm's thinking. But tossing your stuff in front of the house is a dick move. You want a margarita?"

"Skinny spicy, please," Delaney said.

She placed the drink order.

"Why are you getting four margaritas?" her friend asked.

"Pais brought her man."

"Grr. This day! I mean, I'm happy she's found love and all that, but you're single and I'm a hot mess…we need girl time," Delaney lamented.

"It's okay. It will be fun. And I want to check him out," Olive said. She had to admit that focusing on Jack would give her something constructive to do instead of dwelling on her latent mean-spiritedness. Jack seemed like a nice guy but, to be fair, most men did when they first showed up. "Ugh."

"What?" Delaney asked as she winked at the bartender and stole a cherry from the fruit garnishes behind the bar.

"I'm being a super bitch tonight."

"Seriously? I haven't noticed."

"It's probably because I'm suspicious about Jack," Olive confessed.

"Hell, I am too. But mainly because he seems too good to be true," Delaney said. "I mean, he brought Paisley her favorite Cronuts from across town today. And he's sweet."

He was. So why was Olive trying to find a flaw? Was that what she always did? She'd sort of done the opposite of that with Dante…but then he didn't seem to *have* any flaws. Just a regular guy who got superrich and had been waiting for her to turn him into Prince Charming.

She grabbed two of the margaritas and Delaney grabbed the others, then they wove their way through the busy bar back to the table. As they slid into the booth, across from Paisley and Jack, she noticed that Paisley seemed…well, happy. Wasn't that what they all wanted? Why they'd started their business? To find some peace with the past and contentment in their everyday life… Olive sighed. She needed to stop thinking and let it all go.

She'd be nice. And would just keep reinforcing good messages in her mind when the bad ones crept in. They all lifted their drinks. "One for all, all for one."

They clinked them together and took a sip, and Olive felt the vestiges of her bad mood start to slip away. The best thing that had happened to her—besides showing up for community service—was meeting Paisley and Delaney. She never let herself forget it.

"So where is Malcolm? I dragged Jack along because I thought he was coming," Paisley said.

Olive turned to look at Delaney, who chewed her lower lip and then shrugged. "I think we broke up."

"What makes you think that?" Jack asked.

Delaney shook her head.

"The jerk had all her stuff waiting outside of his house when she went home today," Olive said.

"Asshole," Jack bit out. "Sorry about that."

"It's okay. I've been calling him that too," Delaney said. "Anyway, it wasn't working out. I mean, I told Olive this morning I thought it was over."

"Yeah, but wanting it to be over and having him end it the way he did…that's not cool," Paisley stated. "I'm sorry."

"Thanks. He's history though. Tonight is the start of a new Delaney."

*And a new Olive*, Olive thought. She was going to go back to basics. Reinforce her better self while Delaney was starting over. They toasted again and Jack left after the round after getting a text. Paisley walked him out and she and Delaney watched them leave.

"Just once I want to find a man like that," Delaney said. "A man I can trust completely."

"And I want to find a man who makes me trust myself," Olive added.

* * *

Dante walked down the slip in the marina until he got to Max's boat. His friend was already on board and waved at him as he climbed the gangway and joined him. He gave Max a bro hug, stowing the cooler of Inferno Brew below decks.

"I'm so glad you called. I'll deny this if you tell Mia, but the truth is having a baby isn't exactly what I had envisioned," Max said. "I mean, I love being a dad, but it's a lot more than I expected. I'm exhausted and at the same time I feel like I'd die for Rosie. And I'm barely doing anything. Mia does all the heavy lifting, so then I feel like an ass wanting a night out with you."

"There's nothing wrong with needing a break sometimes."

"I suppose you're right," Max said. "So…let's talk about you. You want to cruise the lake or just sit here and drink?"

"Sit and drink," he said. "I need your wisdom."

"Whoa, that's heavy. What's going on?" Max asked. "Hey. Did you trim your beard? I like it."

Dante threw his head back and laughed. "Yeah. I did."

"Thought so. Mia's always saying I'm not observant."

"She so doesn't see you," Dante said. They settled on deck chairs and ordered a pizza from Lou Malnati's.

"What's up?" Max asked after they'd both cracked open a bottle of beer.

"You know me... I mean, you've known all the different parts of my adult life since nerdy college freshman to billionaire entrepreneur."

"Yeah, I have. You've seen me from crazy drunk to serious workaholic to falling hard for Mia..." He narrowed his eyes. "Are you falling for someone?"

Dante took a deep swallow and shook his head. "No. Olive Hayes walked into my office today."

"Oh, hell, no. What'd she want?"

Dante rubbed the back of his neck, looking back toward the skyline of the city as the sun set behind it. What *did* she want? To do her job. That was it. "Kiki hired her company to do a makeover on me and get me ready for the print and video ads she wants to do."

"Did you tell her to get the hell out?" Max asked.

"She didn't recognize me," Dante said.

"Whaaa?"

He glanced over at his friend. Max was the one person in the world who knew how badly that frat party incident with Olive had hurt him. So he was trying to read his friend and figure out what he thought.

"I mean, you were probably one of many she treated that way. I'm not entirely surprised she didn't recognize you. But how are you doing?"

"Like you, I had the same thought about all of that. I'm doing okay...except the makeover, it's bringing out my arrogant playboy tendencies. We had this sort of zing thing when she touched my hand… I think she wants me."

Max finished his beer in one long swallow. "That complicates things. Do you feel the same?"

"It's Olive," he said. "She's like she was when she was bringing me coffees and letting me take the lead on the psych project."

"Yeah, so what are you going to do?" Max asked.

Dante looked over at his friend. Truly one of the best men that Dante had ever met, and he didn't even hesitate to fess up. He couldn't lie to Max. "I thought about sleeping with her, maybe making her believe I wanted a relationship and then, when she starts to like me, dropping her and walking away. Some kind of sexual revenge."

Max reached into the cooler they'd put between their chairs and took out another beer. "You'd be justified if you were still the man you used to be. But you've changed…right? Or do you feel like going back to the love-'em-and-leave-'em phase?"

"I don't want that. I mean, I'm not interested in that kind of life," he said. That was the truth. He liked the peace he'd started to find in his life until Olive Hayes had walked back in and fucked it all up.

"Okay. So now it's just down to revenge or not, right?"

"Yeah. I mean, she hurt a lot of guys, not just me."

"Not just guys. She was in Mia's sorority and was pretty much horrible to her the entire time."

He sighed. Yeah, he remembered that. She'd been a classic mean girl. Nice when she needed something from you but the rest of the time just thought she was better than everyone else and that everyone existed to make her life easier. That quintessential Texas beauty with the sweet Southern accent that could make anyone believe she was genuine until she cut them.

"Has she changed?" Max asked. "After all, I'm not the man I was in college and, frankly, neither are you. Surely she's not like that anymore."

"I'm not sure. She was really nice to her staff and to Kiki. Heck, even to me. Even before I had the haircut and all that."

"That's different," Max said. "But maybe it was just because she works for you."

"That's the problem. I can't trust it until I see more of her. And I can't stop wanting more from her."

"That's natural. She was your fantasy girl in college. You really bought into the fact that she was being mean to protect her softer inside and now she's into you…?"

He groaned at the memory of how he'd spent hours talking about Olive in college. Then he thought about that almost kiss at the elevator and the way she'd been in that moment in the hallway when no one else was around. There'd been some serious sexual tension between them and he'd wanted her. Seriously wanted the woman she was today; he hadn't been thinking of the girl she'd been in college.

"I think so."

"So what are you going to do?"

"That's why I'm here with my wise, married friend," Dante said.

"Hmm. I am wise. You're lucky we're friends," Max quipped, then leaned forward, turning to look at Dante. "But I don't know her. A part of me wants to say go for it. Use her, take what you want and walk away. You deserve that, and so do all the others she hurt."

Dante knew that Max wasn't advocating for revenge. "But?"

"I think it will hurt the man you are if you do it. You've never been as tough as you think you are. Even when you were the king of one-night stands, you cared."

"So, basically, I'm screwed."

"Nah, just take it slow and see what happens. Maybe she'll show you the real woman, good or bad, and then you'll know what to do."

Max's advice stuck with him as they talked about baseball and ate pizza. Mia texted Max about nine, asking when he was coming home, and Dante realized he wanted that. He wanted someone who missed him when he was gone. Revenge wasn't the way he was going to find it. But did he need that to move on?

* * *

Delaney was drunk and determined to salvage this day. So Olive and Paisley weren't surprised when she went home with the bartender she'd been flirting with all evening. But Olive and Paisley both took photos of the bartender as they'd left and, with Delaney's phone tracker, they would be able to find her if things went sideways.

After Delaney left, Olive noticed that Jack was waiting a few feet away for Paisley. Her friend had seemed to find the perfect man. "Looks like your escort is here."

"He can see us both home. I'm not leaving you hanging."

"You're not," Olive said. "My Uber is almost here. I'll be fine."

Paisley waved Jack over to them. "Her ride is on the way."

"Great. We'll wait until it gets here," Jack said.

"Thanks. So what have you been doing tonight?"

"Played B-ball with some friends at the Y. We try to catch up once a month or so. It worked out that Malcolm didn't come tonight," Jack said.

"You were going to ditch them to hang out with us?" Olive asked.

"Yes. Paisley doesn't ask me for much," Jack said, pulling her close and hugging her to his side. Paisley smiled up at her boyfriend and Olive felt almost like a third wheel in that moment.

Jack and Paisley were in tune with each other in a way that Olive hadn't thought existed, but she was witnessing it firsthand. How had she never met a man who she connected with the way that Paisley did with Jack?

Red in the karmic ledger. That was it. She knew it. She was still doing community service for the universe to bring some balance to her life. A car pulled up and she stepped forward, leaning down, surprised to see it was Dante Russo.

"You're probably not my Uber," she said.

"I'm not but I could be," he replied, flashing a grin that made her tingle all over. "I was going to hit the club, but I think I'd rather see you home."

"Is that your ride?" Paisley asked.

"Uh, no, it's my newest client," Olive said.

Paisley and Jack came over. "Hello there."

Olive introduced them and then glanced at her Uber app, noticing that the driver had canceled her ride. Jack and Paisley were going to stay here all night unless she left. "Were you serious about the ride offer?"

"Yes," Dante said.

"Then thank you. He's going to give me a ride home, so you guys can go," Olive told them.

"Text me when you're home," Paisley said, hugging her and whispering in Olive's ear, "He's cute."

She smiled as she stepped back. "I will. Thanks for waiting with me."

She waved goodbye to her friend and got into Dante's car. "Thanks for this. My driver just canceled my ride."

"You're welcome."

She put her seat belt on and he started driving.

"Where to?"

"Uh, I live in the suburbs. Is that too far?"

"Which one? I live in Westmont," he said. "So as long as you're not north, we should be good."

"Well, I live in Westmont too. Just bought a house in January."

"It's a nice place," he said. They made small talk until Swedish House Mafia's "Don't You Worry Child" came on the radio.

She started singing and Dante joined in. While they were both belting out the chorus, all the worries she'd been carrying with her since she'd had that catty moment toward Kiki disappeared. She realized it had been a very long day and that this was what she'd needed.

Singing in a dark car with a guy she had the hots for but barely knew. Maybe she was putting too much pressure on herself—she knew there was no maybe about it. She always did that.

They both were laughing when he pulled into her driveway and turned the radio off. "I love that song."

"It's so much fun," she agreed. "I needed that. Thanks for the ride."

"No worries," he said, turning off the car and getting out.

He was going to open her door. She waited and realized it had been a long time since a guy had done that for her. She didn't need him to, of course, but it just reminded her of the simple courtesies that made others feel better. The kind of gesture that she had made part of her everyday habits to make up for all those times when she'd expected this kind of thing.

"The more I get to know you, the less I think you need my help with this image makeover," she murmured as she took his hand and climbed out of the car.

"Oh, I don't know. Even my best friend noticed I'd trimmed my beard, and guys never notice other men."

She laughed at the way he said that. "You were just a little unruly."

"I like unruly."

"I do too," she said, thinking of him in his flannel shirt and khakis. He'd smartened up for this evening, wearing a pair of dark wash jeans and one of the designer shirts she'd picked out for his new wardrobe.

"You look good tonight," she told him. She wasn't really thinking of the fact that he was her client or that she had decided no more flirting with him. He reminded her of someone, but she couldn't quite put her finger on it. The summer night sky was clear and he was so close, smelling like temptation, and she realized she needed something from him.

Right here…right now.

She leaned in and he tipped his head down. She felt his breath against her cheek and then the brush of his lips against hers. She closed her eyes and realized this was what she'd wanted since she'd seen him with his haircut. He had opened her eyes to the man he was beneath all that scruff and she knew she'd never look at him the same way again.

# Five

Dante hadn't planned on kissing Olive, but singing that song together had dropped both their barriers and she'd smiled at him with such joy that he thought... Well, maybe there was an adult Olive that he had hoped to find. A humble and kind woman.

All of his thoughts dropped away as he fought to keep from deepening the kiss. But she tasted good. Like margaritas and summer and woman. He groaned and pulled her closer, feeling the soft curves of her body against the hardness of his torso and hardening erection.

This was what he'd been craving for more years than he wanted to admit. Olive felt incredible in his arms, tasted better than he'd ever dreamed possible… and affected him more deeply than he wished she would.

But why should that surprise him?

This was Olive Hayes.

*The danger zone.*

Way more so than anything Maverick and Goose had faced in *Top Gun*. He lifted his head. Damn. He wanted more.

He lowered his head before he could overthink this and took a quick deep kiss. He told himself to take it slow, but her mouth had been tempting him for far too long. Her mouth opened under his and her tongue brushed against his, tasting of tequila and lime. He twined her arms around his neck as he intensified the kiss, rubbing his tongue over hers. Then he rocked back, leaned against the side of his car and held her, pretending for a minute that it would be okay to sleep with her.

His body was screaming yes. It was fine to sleep with Olive Hayes even though he'd been debating sexual revenge all day. She felt so damned good in his arms.

He wanted her and denying himself wasn't something he had to do.

But he knew that was a lie.

He had thought about using sex as a tool for revenge, had fucking discussed it with Max this very evening. There was no way he could hook up with her tonight. He set her on her feet and, because he didn't want to stop touching her, drew his hand down her bare arm, enjoying the feel of her soft, smooth skin under his fingers.

"Well, then…" he said.

She licked her lips as she reached up to tuck a strand of hair behind her ear. "Exactly. I think…" She trailed off.

She was caught like he was between this white-hot desire and their professionalism. They worked together. Sleeping together just had HR nightmare written all over it.

"Yeah. So, I'm not going to apologize, because that kiss was incredible. But I will give you my word not to do it again while we are working together," he said. She deserved his best if he wanted to see hers. He knew that part of the problem with her rejection of him in college was that he'd felt unworthy of her. Like somehow it had been okay for him to do all the work on a project in exchange for her smiles and coffee chats. That had been a huge mistake and one he wasn't going to make again.

"I will make the same promise," she whispered, tipping her head to the side and smiling up at him. "Thank you for the ride home and the singing."

"You're welcome," he said.

Olive walked up her drive to her front door and he stayed where he was, leaning against the side of his car as she went inside. She gave him a little wave before the door closed behind her. He took his time walking around to the driver's side of the car.

Dante drove to his house and when he got home, he realized how empty his place felt. He kicked off his shoes and then went to get a large glass of water.

He realized that he'd started to forget where he was in his life. Just because Olive had walked back into his life. All of those years of growth down the drain. His mom believed that events, like his college experience when he'd made a big gesture in front of a crowded group of his peers and was humiliated by Olive, were anchors in life. She thought that there were no good or bad experiences, just growth opportunities.

He wondered what she'd say if he told her about this. He knew he wouldn't. He wasn't into sharing.

He went into his living room, turned on ESPN and just stared at the screen when he got an idea for another of his "beer casts," as he called his audio feeds Kiki used for their radio ads.

He muted the television and then closed his eyes, turning on the voice recording app on his phone.

"The heat of summer is making me hot and restless. Like I am on fire, and the city feels that way too. I need something to draw me out of the Inferno that I'm walking through each day. I have to remind myself of where I am. That this is just the season of heat and soon we'll be into that time of cozy comfort."

He stopped recording. Not sure that was anything

he wanted to share. His phone pinged and he glanced at the text from IDG Brand Imaging. Olive?

Thanks again for everything tonight.

You're welcome. Just sitting here staring at the empty night and wishing maybe we both weren't so conscientious.

Me too. But I know I'll be glad in the morning.

He wasn't so sure he would be, but he wasn't about to put that out there.

Me too.

Well...good night, Dante.

Good night, Olive.

*Good night, Olive.* Words he'd never thought he'd say. He knew that the kiss and everything else with her was a slippery slope. There was no way to divorce himself from the past. It had shaped him into the man he was today and a lot of that stemmed directly from her. He wondered if she'd ever connect him to the boy she'd known in college. He wasn't too worried about it; he was still trying to take the higher ground and be okay with it.

Granted, he still had the anger and some of the bitterness she stirred in him. He saw glimpses of this new woman as well as some of the familiar Olive, but a different part of him was excited he was talking to her and pissed that she could still make him feel that way.

The inferno wasn't just the heat of summer. Those circles of hell were torture, and what was more torturous than being shown the woman he'd once wanted and finding her suddenly accessible to him? He knew he needed to get rid of those thoughts and that feeling that he could somehow do anything with her and remain aloof.

He couldn't. That kiss tonight had proven it. He would take Max's advice and, of course, keep his distance, but see if there was more of this new Olive than the old one.

Olive told herself that she was just excited to get back to work, but after ten days of not seeing Dante, she had to admit part of those butterflies were because she'd be in his presence again. She'd set up some media training, but he hardly needed that. Now they were meeting at a downtown studio she'd booked for the afternoon. She wanted a chance to see how he performed on camera before his first interview, which was the next morning on the local NBC affiliate's morning show.

She checked her watch again, realizing that only

five minutes had gone by since the last time she'd checked. It was 9:05 a.m. and they weren't meeting until 2:00 p.m. She needed to focus.

"Ugh. Did you see this?" Delaney walked into her office with her phone screen turned toward Olive.

She took the phone from the other woman and skimmed it. It was *Wend-Z City*. Chicago's answer to *TMZ*. The site had videos and an online zine that mainly covered big gossip from A-listers and reality TV stars but also kept tabs on Chi-Town's social scene.

### Mad, Bad Delaney Strikes Again

*The dish soap heiress apparently doesn't know when to let go. After being dumped by Malcolm Quell, she was seen on his doorstep arguing with the butler to try to get back in. Girl, please, show some dignity. It's time to let go.*

Olive cringed and looked over at Delaney, who looked ready to explode. "Okay. I mean, it's not the worst thing she's said about you."

"No, it's not. But for one, it's not true. And secondly, I wasn't dumped."

"Uh...technically—"

"Stop! I thought you were my friend," Delaney huffed.

"I am. So, what is the truth? You know we have

a very good attorney on retainer and we can sue if she's made this up," Olive said. Delaney had moved in with her three days after...well, after she'd kissed Dante. But had moved back out because in her words, "The suburbs are *boring*." She'd bought a condo overlooking Lake Michigan and had been living there since.

"Who are we suing?" Paisley asked as she walked into Olive's office.

"*Wend-Z*. They've printed some outrageous things about Delaney," Olive said, handing her the phone.

Paisley read it and then shrugged. "I'd say ignore it. Did you see the next story? Hollywood celebrity Sean O'Neill hasn't been spotted since New Year's Eve. Insiders confirm that producers on his latest project are getting nervous."

"He's like—what?—a billionaire and has won like every award that they give out. Maybe he's ready for a change," Delaney said. "He should get a real job. Can we please get back to me?"

Olive smiled to herself. She didn't disagree with Delaney's assessment. Sean O'Neill was more famous for his bad-boy antics and scandalous affairs than for his acting roles in recent years. She thought he needed a break from his lifestyle and, more than likely, a purpose.

"What about you? Is this not true?" Paisley asked. "Slander is really hard to prove in court."

"It's partially true, but I wasn't there because I want him back. He won't give me back Stanley."

"I thought you were both splitting custody of the dog," Paisley said.

"We were. Except when I went to pick him up, the butler wouldn't give him to me and said that Malcolm and his new ho had taken him to Paris for the weekend. Don't even get me started about that," Delaney said.

"We won't. Okay, so we need the lawyer for the dog custody." Olive scowled. "He can't keep your dog from you. I mean, you bought him. Stanley is your forever man."

"He is. Which, of course, I told the douchebag and so now he's keeping him hostage. I mean, I only agreed to split custody because Stanley, that traitorous sweetie, actually likes Malcolm."

"We can figure this out. When will he be back in the country?" Paisley asked.

"Not sure. I can't call the private airport to find out since *Wend-Z* is on to me," Delaney said.

"I can," Olive said. She picked up the phone, dialed the private airport and had a quick conversation about Malcolm's flight plans. "He's leaving for Barbados tonight."

"The hell he is!" Delaney fumed.

"That's what they said. Want me to call his assistant and see if I can get the scoop?" Olive asked.

"Nah. None of my friends are allowed to have contact with anyone in his employment."

"Why?"

"He filed a restraining order against me," Delaney admitted.

"Okay, you should have led with that," Paisley said. "I'm going to call the attorney and then we are going to get this sorted."

Paisley left Olive's office and Delaney followed her. Olive was fit to be tied. Stanley was the sweetest French bulldog in the world and Delaney had gotten him after a particularly bad year. This was so unfair.

But a part of her wondered if it was that karmic ledger of Delaney's. Her past wasn't as littered with broken people the way that Olive's was, but she'd still lived her life with little regard for anyone else.

Her phone rang, disrupting her thoughts. She glanced at the caller ID and saw that it was Dante. Her pulse sped up and her heart was beating a little faster. She patted down her hair and realized he couldn't see her. *Just answer the phone.*

"Hello, Dante."

"Hiya, Olive. I need a favor. I am going to the charity fundraiser tonight at the Art Institute and my date just had to cancel. I was wondering if you'd go with me."

She told herself it was just a work thing, but he'd asked her out. On a date. It had been too long since she'd been on one and it was Dante. *Be cool.* She pulled up her calendar on her computer and saw that she was free. She googled the event and noticed that they were doing a red carpet, so it would be good for Dante to test out his new look and media prowess. "I will. I see there is a red carpet. So we can prep you for that. I'll meet you there."

"Sounds good. See you this afternoon," he said, hanging up.

He'd kept the call all business, which was perfectly reasonable. Just because she kept thinking of the way his lips had felt against hers at odd times didn't mean that he felt the same. In fact, she shouldn't feel that way, either, but as soon as she'd marked him off limits, it seemed her mind and her imagination couldn't stop thinking about him.

Dante realized despite the ten days they'd been apart, he wasn't really as chill toward Olive as he wanted to be. He had written off the kiss as desire fulfillment from college. But seeing her now looking... Well, he knew she'd call it professional, but there was something so feminine in the way she dressed that he'd hardened when he'd seen her.

She gave him a little wave as she walked over to him. He couldn't help standing taller and trying to impress her. That, he knew, was not a smart thing to do.

"Kiki tells me that the morning show asked you to do a reveal," Olive said. "I think with your charm, you could pull it off, but it could also seem cheesy, so I'd say make sure you do it on your own terms."

Dante already had a few qualms about doing a "reveal," so this wasn't really helping. She smelled like spring despite the heat of summer, which was distracting him and reminding him of the fact that his shirt had smelled like Olive after he'd kissed her. And that had made him remember how good she'd tasted.

"Do you want me to meet you down there?"

He was pretty confident he could go on as himself if it had something to do with some sort of here's-the-guy-behind-the-voice thing. But if Olive wanted to meet him at the studio at 6:00 a.m., who was he to say no?

"Sure. I wasn't planning on allowing anything too corny. But as you're the professional, it will be good to have you on hand."

"No problem. Okay, so let's come up with some scenarios that would work for you and see how it looks on camera. This is Lucas, a film student, who will be filming you, and Courtney is a director and she's going to be in charge here."

"Nice to meet you both," Dante said.

"Same. What do you want me to do?"

Kiki and Olive gave the kid some direction and Dante looked over at the props Kiki had brought along. The Inferno Brewing backdrop and the pony keg and six-packs of their summer brew.

"From what I understand, you generally do your audio stuff off the cuff. Do you want to try that with the video?" Olive asked.

"Yeah. I mean, Kiki didn't write anything for me, did you?"

"Nope. You're much better when I don't put words in your mouth," Kiki said. "But remember the message. Summer's hot and there's one man who knows how to deal with the heat."

"Satan?"

"I thought you said not to call you that," Kiki said with a wink.

"I'd steer away from Satan references," Olive suggested. "I think Inferno is hot enough."

"Agreed," Dante said. "So what do I do?"

"Just be yourself. Kiki and I will stand behind the camera, so look toward us and talk about your product."

Olive and Kiki stood behind Lucas. They wanted him to create some sort of reveal that would make tomorrow morning's news show go more easily. Dante walked where he thought he might be out of shot. And started talking.

"Hello, Chicagoland. You and me, we go way back," he began and then slowly walked forward, looking at the camera lens as he did so. "I might not look familiar, but my voice might be stirring memories and making you think of summer days. Maybe taking a six-pack of beer down to the Bean or Lake

Michigan. I'm the CEO and founder of Inferno Brewing, Dante Russo."

He stopped talking, lifted one of the bottles of beer and smiled at the camera.

"Love it. Boss, you are *killing* it! That's perfect," Kiki exalted. "Is there a way to see it back?"

"Yes. Give me a minute and I'll get it cued up for you," Lucas said, going over to Courtney.

Olive walked to Dante as Kiki and the film students worked together.

"What'd you think?" he asked her. Very aware that he wanted to impress her with every detail of his life. If she ever remembered him as Danny Russo, he wanted her to be blown away by how far he'd come. How much he'd changed.

"I liked it. I really don't have many suggestions other than maybe you use your new audio slogan before you step onto the screen. That way viewers will already hear your message once before it hits the airwaves."

"Good idea," he said. "I'm sure Kiki will be all over that."

"I'm sure she will. She's so...clever," Olive remarked, glancing across at the other woman.

"She is," Dante said, trying to tell himself that there was no way Olive was jealous of Kiki. This was Olive Hayes. The woman who had everything and let everyone know it. "She's like a kid sister to me."

"She is?"

"Yeah. She's been working for me for the last few years, but she was part of the team before we hit big," Dante explained.

"You seem to have found the right people for every stage of your career," Olive said. "First Kiki and now me."

He arched his eyebrow. "Definitely. But just to be clear, I don't think of you as my sister."

"I should hope not," she said, winking at him.

"Come and look at this," Kiki said, waving them over.

They had set up a laptop and connected the camera to it, and Dante realized he was nervous to see himself on video. He tended to avoid watching himself— a holdover from the days when he had been insecure and not really liked his appearance.

Dante heard his voice and then, a few moments later, he appeared on screen. And he had that moment of not really recognizing himself in the new clothes, swaggering into frame and talking to the camera like he knew he had something to say that everyone wanted to hear.

It had been a very long time coming but Dante saw in that image the man he'd always wanted to be. He was on a path to realizing a dream he'd harbored since he'd been on his own. He realized that there was only one way to achieve it and that was to keep looking forward.

There was no time to dwell on the past or on revenge. He wasn't going to even the odds or make that decade past situation better for himself. He nodded as he heard the others talking but he wasn't paying attention. It was ironic that it had taken seeing himself on the laptop to realize how far he'd come and that he didn't want to go backward.

"Let's do it again. Olive suggested I use our summer slogan before I step into frame," Dante said.

"Good idea."

He shot two or three more takes but everyone thought he'd aced it. And as he said goodbye to Olive, he realized, despite the fact they were going on a work date that evening, he was looking forward to it.

# Six

Olive had debated what to wear to the event and settled on a buttercup-yellow suit with wide-leg trousers and a matching jacket. She left the jacket open and wore a complementary bikini top with wide triangle cups that provided ample coverage. Olive styled it with her favorite pair of Louboutins and her favorite Chanel clutch. She was staying at Delaney's new condo for the night since it was in the city and not too far from the Art Institute.

She came out of her bedroom, debating how she should style her shoulder-length locks. "Should I put my hair up?"

Delaney glanced over and let out a wolf whistle.

Olive styled a few poses for her friend and winked at her. "Thanks. Hair?"

"I'd leave it down. You look so elegant and sophisticated, but also like it's just your natural style and you're not trying."

"That's what I was going for. I mean, it is a work do and not a date, but it is also with Dante…"

"I'm so bummed I didn't get to meet him," Delaney said. "Is he as hot as his voice sounds?"

Olive nodded, chewing her lower lip, wondering how much she should share with her friend. But then immediately decided everything. When she started hiding things, she ended up on a downward spiral.

"Hotter. Honestly, I'm struggling to keep from fantasizing about him," she admitted.

"Wow. Why struggle?" Delaney asked. "It's not like he's your boss or anything."

"Maybe so, but he *is* a client. So we both decided to just play it cool until our business relationship ends."

"Why did you both decide that? Did something happen?" Delaney turned on the couch and leaned against the back of it.

"We shared a kiss," Olive admitted, trying to sound like it was nothing. Just a normal everyday occurrence.

"Okay. I kiss my grandma, so was it *just* a kiss?"

"Well, when you put it like that," she said, "it was so much more than that. He's…so unexpected. He's super cool and nice and funny and all these things that I know must be genuine."

"But?"

"There's something about him that stirs up old feelings. I mean, until I arranged for his haircut and beard trim, I didn't notice it. What if I'm doing that thing I do where I like him because of who I made him into?" Olive asked, coming over to perch on the arm of the chair next to her friend.

Delaney put her hand on Olive's shoulder. "What if you are? I guess just seeing where things go and not sleeping together while you're working with him is a good idea. Is it giving you a chance to figure out what's going on in your head?"

Delaney had a point. She was just being chill and letting things happen naturally. It had been a minute since she'd done that. She normally just dived head-first into affairs that lasted a few weeks or months because she hadn't trusted herself to let anyone in. That, she immediately knew, was a lie. She hadn't felt like she'd done enough to actually be loveable.

"I want to be good enough for Dante, Dellie."

"You are," Delaney said, standing up and coming around to hug her. "When are you going to stop punishing yourself for your mistakes?"

Olive didn't know. She had so much to make up for and just didn't feel like she'd done enough. Would she ever? "I had a really mean moment the first day I met him."

"What? What did you do?"

"Nothing to anyone. Just thought some unkind thoughts," Olive murmured, remembering her jealousy of Kiki, which Dante had totally neutralized today when he'd mentioned he thought of the other woman as a sister.

"What? I do that constantly. Like when you walked in here, I thought, *That bitch. She looks way too good*," Delaney said, smiling at her. "It's okay to think stuff like that."

She smiled back because she knew that Delaney was trying to make her feel better, but Olive remembered her old way of thinking. How those thoughts grew into a full-blown royal mindset. Where she thought that everyone existed to make her life easier. "Thanks, bitch."

"Ha! See. It feels good every once in a while to say those kinds of things. But you have to balance it out. Like your karmic ledger theory. So to make up for being so mean about how hot you look, I will tell you I love you."

"I know you do," Olive said, hugging her friend back. Her watch pinged and she glanced down to see that the alarm she'd set to remind her when to leave was going off. "I have to go. Wish me luck."

"*Luck*. Not that you need it," Delaney added. "You're going to make him regret he said he wanted to keep things all business!"

"Thanks. See ya later," Olive said.

"Or not. Maybe you'll get extra lucky!" her friend told her, waving goodbye from the couch.

On the drive to the Art Institute, Olive couldn't help mulling over everything Delaney had said. It had comforted her to think that there was a way she could make up for how she'd been in the past, but another part of her realized the universe might not operate that way. She tried every day to be a better person, but there were times when it felt more like one step forward, two steps backward.

Traffic built the closer they got to the Art Institute and she had the Uber driver drop her off around the corner, knowing she could walk there quicker than he could drive. She worked her way to the front, saw the media and lights and red carpet. She stood off to the side, watching for Dante, and then she saw him.

She already loved the way he looked in his casual clothes, but holy smokes, the sight of him in that custom-tailored tuxedo that fit his tall frame and broad shoulders to perfection made her heart stutter in her chest. He skimmed the people, looking for her, and she held her breath and whispered a prayer that some might say she had no right to ask, but just once she wanted to be good enough.

The tux was made to fit so, of course, wasn't really choking him, but he felt like it was. It was safe to say that he wasn't loving this part of the make-over. Mia was originally supposed to be his date for tonight because she'd wanted a night out after Max had met him for drinks, but had had to cancel because the baby was sick and, even though she didn't say it directly, she hadn't wanted to leave little Rosie at home alone with Max. Mia was super overprotective of their daughter and had tried to explain it to him, but in the end had confessed she just wasn't ready to leave the baby.

He'd got it and it had worked to his advantage because it had given him an excuse to ask Olive to join him tonight. He scanned the small crowd milling around the red carpet—a line had formed for everyone to enter—and then he saw her. She looked like summer in her yellow suit and, when she turned, waving at him and starting to walk to him, he felt a rush of lust go through him.

She moved with that unconscious grace that had first drawn his eye all those years ago, but also in a way that was so feminine and womanly, she couldn't help but attract attention. Her outfit was elegant and sexy at the same time. He noticed other heads turn, and she had that beguiling smile on her face.

For the first time he noticed the warmness she exuded. Her expression was welcoming, friendly, and it wasn't just directed at him. That was new. She'd never smiled at everyone in the past. Her genuine smiles had been saved for the few who had graced her inner circle.

He tucked that knowledge away in the back of his

mind. But a part of him was happier than he should be to realize that she was different now.

He wanted to spot more differences, and hoped he wasn't fooling himself into seeing what he wanted. But for tonight he wasn't going to worry over it. This was a chance for both of them to explore their attraction with some safety limits in place.

"Hello, gorgeous," she said, mimicking Barbra Streisand from that old movie she was in.

"Hello, beautiful," he returned. "I wish I'd thought to ditch the bow tie and shirt."

"You are killing it with them on, so I'm glad you didn't," she said.

"Good to know. Kiki wants me to make sure they know I'm the CEO of Inferno Brewing, but I'm not sure how to do that," Dante muttered.

"No problem. I'll make sure they know. We didn't go over it, but do you know how to stand when they take your photo?"

"Well, I have been standing for ages," he said.

"No, I mean sort of pose. We should have done a few test angles, but I wasn't anticipating this kind of event so soon. I'd say just look the camera straight-on and then try a couple of side poses maybe with your hand in your pocket. But make sure you tuck the tail of the jacket behind your arm to showcase your body."

"Okay. Anything else?"

"Just smile and, oh, do that brooding stare thing you did this afternoon," she said.

"I have no idea what you are talking about."

She turned, sort of pursed her lips and then angled her chin down but looked up at him. "Something like that."

A jolt of pure lust went through him again, and he clenched his hand into a fist to keep from reaching for her.

"Your turn," she said.

He tried it but felt dumb. She started laughing, so he was pretty sure he hadn't done it right. "So not that."

"Just smile. You have the best smile I've ever seen," she murmured.

His lips quirked. "The *best* you say?"

"I do. Don't let it go to your head, but I'm pretty sure if Sean O'Neill doesn't resurface you could totally go to Hollywood and take his place."

"I like where I am," he said, touching her hand.

She tipped her head to the side. "Me too."

"Next."

The pages monitoring the red carpet called them forward. There was only one couple in front of them. He wanted to keep talking to her.

Olive stepped aside. "I'm going to go work the reporters. They will call out and ask you questions. Just try to tie it back to Inferno Brewing and your summer release."

"I'll try," he said.

She moved away and he watched the sway of her hips and noticed how long her legs looked in that stunning outfit, which led to how they'd feel wrapped around his hips.

"You're next, sir."

Dante took a deep breath as the red carpet attendant gestured for him to step forward, and reluctantly turned away from Olive after noting she seemed to know most of the photographers and the news folks in attendance.

"Name?"

"Dante Russo, Inferno Brewing," he said.

"Good to meet you. Your summer brew is getting me through this heat wave," the man said. "So if you could make sure to pose in front of the logo at the end, we'd appreciate it."

"I'm happy to." Dante walked onto the red carpet and the cameras turned toward him. He was blinded by the flashes and realized this wasn't his scene. But he knew he had a job to do so he smiled and answered questions, all the while wishing that Olive was with him. When he got to the end, she was waiting, and he waved her over so that they could pose together in front of the charity logo.

Dante looked down at her and she winked at him, putting her arm around his waist. He put his arm around her too, and damn him if she didn't fit perfectly under his arm against his side. They both grinned at the photographer and then moved toward the entrance of the event.

He had to get out his invitation and, once they were inside, realized that he was still tense. It was a combination of his attraction for Olive, adrenaline from the red carpet stuff, and the fact that he was out with the one woman who'd once told him she'd let the population die before she was seen in public with him.

He was having those unbidden feelings again— the *revenge* ones—and then she smiled at him. "Glad that's over now, so we can just relax. You want to find our table and I'll go and get our drinks?"

But this wasn't the same Olive. She was acting like he'd seen Mia do with Max. Like they were a couple. Dante rubbed the back of his neck. He couldn't let himself stay in that mindset, and a few minutes apart would probably help.

"Yeah. Jack and Coke, please," he said.

"Meet back here?"

He nodded as she disappeared into the crowd. He was playing a game that he wasn't sure he should be. Maybe he needed to bench himself, because he was very afraid he was going to hurt Olive and he didn't want to do that.

Olive and Dante were at a table for eight with three other couples that all knew each other. They were nice, but after they'd exchanged some small talk there wasn't much really to say.

She thought this was her chance to learn a bit more about Dante. Like Delaney had mentioned, she was in a safety zone. She could ask all the questions she wouldn't if they were dating.

"You mentioned you grew up in the Midwest?" she asked.

"I did," he said, raising his eyebrows. "What's this?"

"Just trying to get to know you better outside of work."

"Oh. So have you changed your mind about all that?"

She shrugged. "Maybe. I mean, no. I really am trying to be a better person."

"And not sleeping with me will make you one?"

"When did we decide to sleep together?" she asked.

"If that kiss had gone on a second longer—" he reached under the table, putting his hand on her thigh "—or was it just me?"

Shivers went through her. Her breasts felt fuller and she felt her heart beat a little heavier. She wanted to shift closer to him on her chair, knowing that would force his touch higher on her thigh.

"It wasn't just you," she admitted, putting her hand on his thigh too.

"I suspected. But my mama always said don't make assumptions."

She nodded. "Mine too. She's full of advice."

"Like what?" he asked as the waiter refilled their drinks.

"A smile will open any door."

After the waiter left, he arched one eyebrow at her. "Let's see the door opener."

Olive tossed her hair and squared her shoulders before she turned and gave him her pageant smile. The one that always got results.

"Not bad. I'd definitely hold the door for you."

She laughed and shook her head. "What advice did *you* get?"

"Be yourself and people will respect you for it."

"That's good advice," she said.

A shadow crossed his face. "Unless you're a nerd," he muttered.

"Which you clearly aren't," she said.

"And if I were?" he asked, his tone suddenly turning serious.

He'd been flirty and seductive and now…his entire demeanor had changed. Something else was going on here. But she couldn't think when he was so close.

"Well then I'd say they were right. I like who you are," she said. "There was a time in my life when I wouldn't have been able to admit that."

"Why not?" he asked, taking a long swallow of his drink.

"I just didn't see the good around me," she confessed, realizing this wasn't the conversation she wanted to have. "I would have said you were a beer drinker, but Jack?"

"Oh, I drink a lot of beer," he said. "What about you?"

"Beer for cookouts, baseball games and Oktoberfest, but I do like mixed drinks and wine too… Actually, I have yet to try anything that I don't like—wait, except for sambuca shots. I don't care for them."

"No one likes sambuca. That's a late-night-at-the-bar kind of drink," he said.

"Yeah it is. Sometimes I close them down. Well, back in my early twenties," she clarified.

"Me too. Junior year of college especially. Then, once I hit twenty-four, I was like, 'I'm not doing a shot of something gross.' Guess I finally matured," he said.

She smiled as she thought that was about when she'd started to wise up to life and what she really wanted hers to be. "Me too."

The emcee for the charity started the program, which was talking about their work while the meal was served. Every once in a while, Dante would lean over and ask her a question.

She learned that they both preferred the beach over mountain vacations. He liked old-school rock and the Beastie Boys. He even rapped a bit of "Paul Revere" for her. She told him that she was a die-hard Miley Cyrus fan, but her favorites were the Hannah Montana songs.

That, he gruffly conceded to liking too.

When the program ended, and dinner was over, they opened the bar. Then a deejay came on, and she held her breath. Dancing...did she want to stay for that? Yes.

"Up for some dancing? Or is that too personal for a business date?" he asked as the others at their table got up and moved to the bar.

"I was just wondering that. I think we're both mature, so unless one of us suggests sambuca, we should be okay."

He shook his head and laughed. "Agreed."

The deejay played "Happy" by Pharrell, and Dante grabbed her hand and they hit the dance floor. And as she danced with him, she realized how much she'd changed since twenty-two. It was funny that Dante had mentioned maturing. She'd forgotten how far she'd come from the girl she'd been until this moment. She'd thought the changes had been small but they might be more significant.

She danced alongside him, knowing she'd changed a lot from the woman who used to hate herself and everyone else. She was glad to be where she was now and with this man.

At the end of the night when they had danced to every song and she'd drunk more wine than she should have, the deejay played "Closing Time" by Semisonic and Dante pulled her close and leaned down to whisper in her ear.

"Tell me I'm not the only one craving a shot of sambuca."

She laughed and realized that she actually was starting to get into Dante. *For real*.

# Seven

Beer fest weekend arrived and the entire team loaded into Inferno Brewing vans and headed up to Milwaukee. Dante remembered the first year he'd gone and how it had been the first time he'd been a sponsor in a big tent instead of one of the many novelty craft brewers. Today was another one of those big moments. His brewing company was the head-lining beer at the festival and he would be featured on the main stage, introducing one of the key music acts.

And Olive was coming with them. She was meeting him at the festival site to help him with how to project his image, though he felt like he was already pretty close to not really needing her advice anymore. Yet at the same time he was reluctant to end the relationship. After the charity event at the Art Institute something had changed between them. He no longer saw her as just the woman from his past; there was much more to her and he enjoyed every part of it. The more he got to know her, the more he realized he should probably come clean. But he had no idea how to bring up their past connection.

Inferno Brewing staff were all wearing the promotional T-shirts they'd had designed for the event, and they had a flight with all nine circle beers. They got to the festival grounds around nine and Dante supervised getting everything set up. He was what he liked to call a hands-on manager and what Kiki insisted was a micromanager. But since he'd started the company on his own, it was hard to let go. Especially when he was at a big event like this one.

"Remember we can only give T-shirts to people over the drinking age," he said. "We have the stuffed devil bears for kids and anyone underage."

There were affirmations from his staff.

"Let's have fun today," he said.

"Wow, what a pep talk," Kiki quipped. "Did you write it yourself?"

He turned and smirked at her. "As a matter of fact, I did. My PR person was on a date last night and unavailable."

"Good for her," Kiki said with a grin as she walked past him.

"Could you use an extra pair of hands?" Olive asked. She was wearing a pair of white shorts that ended midthigh and a Second Circle T-shirt that she'd knotted on the side. Large dark-framed sunglasses covered her eyes and she had on an Inferno Brewing black baseball cap. She was decked out in his merchandise and logo, and he couldn't help feeling a bit possessive and turned on when he saw her.

"I think we've got it covered, but if you want to help, I could use someone on the stuffed bears. They always go fast," he said.

"They are super cute," Olive said. "I'm surprised that you thought of it."

"Why?" he asked.

"Oh, I guess because you're a guy," she said. "Which makes me sound really not nice. I just meant it's a cute giveaway and really something that a lot of other companies aren't doing."

"It's fair. I noticed that most of the swag that was for underage people were Koozies or beer-bottle-shaped merch, and I don't think many parents are going to want their kids to keep that long term. But a beer bear…that had possibilities. Since I was using the circles of hell, the devil bear seemed logical, and it's cute not scary," he said, explaining his thinking as he walked her over to the large barrels where the bears were kept.

"I like it and it feels genuine, like everything else you do," she said. "So what am I doing here?"

*Genuine.* Yeah, he was, except for the fact that he hadn't mentioned they'd known each other in college. He knew he was going to have to come clean with her. Soon. But for today, he was going to focus on beer fest. He gestured to the front of their tent where he had two staff members stationed at each of the three entrances. Their tent was large, air-conditioned, and set up so that legal drinkers and the underaged were separated when they entered. Parents and children were sent into a middle section that both of the paths could service.

"After everyone is sorted as they enter, they can stop at each of these stations and play a game, win prizes, et cetera. Like I said, I could use you here to hand out the devil bears to the kids and anyone else that wins one on the wheel. We also have the beer beach towels and beach balls. Use your judgment about divvying up the prizes. If a kid really wants a bear, don't say no. I want them to all leave with a positive experience of the day."

"Okay, I can do that," Olive said. "What will you be doing?"

"Dispensing beer over there at the free tasting. If you get tired of doing this, just say the word and I'll send in reinforcements," he said.

"I'm sure I'll manage just fine. I've been enjoying hearing about this event. Maybe we grab lunch together and go over your outfit and message for to-night?"

"I'd love that. I'll see you around one?" he suggested, trying to be casual though he felt anything other than chill. He hadn't forgotten that he wanted to see if she'd changed, and more and more lately it seemed she had.

The Olive he'd known in college wouldn't have even shown up until the main event, and then she would have had her entourage around her. This woman seemed so different; he wanted to believe the change was real, but a part of him was afraid to trust himself and to trust her.

Maybe telling her about their shared past would be the first step to that? He wasn't convinced. Not yet.

Dante left her side to stand behind the taps at the beer station. He loved the smell of his beer and he looked at his staff, who were all nervous and excited as they waited for the event to begin.

Olive hadn't expected to enjoy working in a beer tent. It was contra to everything she'd thought about herself and used to define who she was. But the kids were all so cute and the people she worked with friendly. The parents were all grateful to have something for their kids who might not enjoy a day of just beer tents.

She couldn't help glancing over at Dante more than once. He was in his element. Despite the wardrobe changes and makeover she'd orchestrated for him, she knew that what really drew her eyes was him. There was something about the easy way he talked to his staff and to consumers…the way he made everyone feel welcome. She couldn't deny he looked hot in his jeans and Inferno Brewing tee, but it was more than his body that attracted her. His voice was loud in the tent and though she couldn't hear his words, she could tell from his tone and from the smile on his face that he was enjoying himself.

Olive overheard comments about the hunky CEO, several of them mentioning that he was hotter than they'd pictured when they'd heard his audio ads. That made her smile. She'd done that. But then, she'd been working with a great model. It hadn't taken much polish to bring out the best in Dante.

He noticed her staring at him and waved, and she waved back before turning away. She'd never been this open in a relationship. Probably precisely because it *wasn't* one. They were working together and, though there was a lot of chemistry between them, neither was willing to jeopardize their professional relationship, so that was making it easier for her to drop her guard.

In fact, she hadn't realized how much easier until this moment.

"Excuse me."

A small hand tugged on the hem of her shorts and Olive looked down into a pair of big brown eyes ringed by the longest lashes she'd ever seen. She stooped down to be on level with the little girl. "My brother really wanted one of these bears…but he got the ball instead."

She noticed the little boy standing slightly behind but next to his sister. "Well then, let's get him a bear."

Olive stood, went over to the barrel and grabbed a bear out, taking it back over to the boy and handing it to him.

"Thank you," he said.

"No problem."

When she stood back up she noticed the mom was watching her. "Thank you for that."

"Like I said, it was no problem at all. Have a good day."

The family moved on and she heard the mother compliment her daughter on asking and reminded both of her children that it was always okay to ask for something you wanted. Olive felt that twinge deep inside. The part of her that hoped one day to be a mom. But she still wasn't sure she was ready for that. It all went back to being a person who liked herself. She was getting closer.

Actually working with Dante was helping her see herself in a new way. There had been a time when she would have walked away before helping at an event like this. She would have told that kid no too. Not out of meanness but because she'd been raised that you took what was given. And that was it. So Olive had always made sure she got what she wanted.

But that no longer applied to her. And she still had regrets about the way she'd been.

"Ready for an early lunch?" Dante asked, coming up behind her. He was so close that she felt the heat of his body along her back, and she closed her eyes and started to lean toward him before stopping herself.

This lust was getting out of control. As much as she was afraid to tell him he didn't need her professional services anymore because then she wouldn't have a built-in reason to see him. She also couldn't wait much longer to be able to explore what was happening between them.

"Yes," she said.

He slipped his hand in hers and led the way out of the tent. "Wow. I can't believe how long the line is to get into our tent."

"I can. You are in high demand."

"Thanks to your makeover and Kiki's marketing campaign," Dante said. "I mean, no one would have shown up for the lumberjack."

"I'm not so sure about that. You were pretty cute as a lumberjack," Olive teased.

"Oh, really?" he asked, tugging her out of the crowd to a quiet spot between the Inferno Brewing trucks. "I wouldn't have thought I was your type."

"I don't think I have a type," she admitted. Not

anymore. "Or if I do, it's more a confident man who knows what he wants."

"Well, I am that," he said, putting his arm on the van behind her and shielding her from the rest of the crowd as he leaned in.

He smelled a little bit like Inferno's summer brew and a lot like Dante. The man she'd come to fantasize about every night. She tipped her head back, very aware that she was crossing a line she'd promised herself she wouldn't cross.

"I can tell," she murmured.

"I'm glad," he said. "I've been trying to flex my muscles each time you glance my way—"

She started laughing and he stopped talking, just arching one eyebrow at her. "What?"

"You don't flex. To be honest, you don't need to."

"You like the way I look?" he asked.

She put her hand on his chest. "Yes, Dante. From the first moment I saw your haircut, you took my breath away."

"From the first moment I laid eyes on you, you did the same to me," he said.

He leaned in and she felt the brush of his breath against her cheek and parted her lips. Wanting to kiss him again with every fiber of her being. It had been so long since she'd been this close to him. Two weeks to be exact. Since that moment at the Art Institute when the deejay had played "Closing Time" and she'd realized she wanted to go home with Dante.

And had chickened out.

She didn't want to chicken out again, but if she did this…

He put his hand on the side of her neck. "I made you a promise, Olive. That's the only reason I'm going to step back. I want you to know I'm a man of my word."

He started to turn away and she caught his hand. "What if I said I'd changed my mind?"

Dante looked back at her. He had never been more tempted by anything in his life. He looked down at their joined hands, and it was all he could do not to tug her into his arms and take the kiss that he'd been craving since he'd seen her watching him in the tent.

"Dante! There you are. I need you in the tent. One of the executives from Brewing Energy Worldwide is here and he wants to talk to you," Larry said.

Larry was his second-in-command of operations. The Brewing Energy Worldwide executive was a big deal. They'd been trying to get a distribution deal in Europe and this could be the key. "I'll be right there."

"Don't wait. This is big," Larry said.

"I got it," he muttered, glancing back at Olive.

She just gave him that soft smile. "Go on. We can talk later," she said.

He hesitated, knowing that moments like this weren't to be ignored, but at the same time he couldn't risk his business for Olive. Biting back a groan, he nodded and followed Larry. He took a few moments as he walked through the tent to pull in all of the confidence in himself that he needed to sell the executive on Inferno Brewing.

"This is Dante Russo, the CEO and founder of Inferno Brewing," Larry said. "Dante, this is Jeff Werner from Brewing Energy Worldwide."

"Jeff, nice to meet you. Have you tried our summer brew?" Dante asked.

"I have. Very refreshing. I'd love to talk to you about distribution. My assistant tells me you've made a few calls to my office," Jeff said.

"That's correct," Dante admitted.

"I'm sorry I didn't have the time to take your calls. The truth is we hear from a dozen or so new breweries each week and we can't distribute them all," Jeff said.

"I get it," Dante said. "I'm glad you were able to stop by today and at least sample our product."

"I am too. Makes me realize I was missing out on some really good beer. I want to make it up to you. Can you join me for lunch and we can talk business?"

Dante didn't want to let Jeff go without a discussion, but he had made plans with Olive. "Yes. I can do that. Give me a minute to let my staff know."

"Take your time," the other man said.

He waved Kiki over to him. "I'm sorry to do this but I was supposed to have lunch with Olive. She's over by the vans outside the tent. Will you let her know that I had to take a business meeting? That I'll meet her back here after."

"Sure thing, boss," Kiki said. "I'll take her to lunch for you so we can compare notes about you."

He shook his head at his marketing manager. "No gossiping."

"Oh, I won't tell her anything you don't want her to know," Kiki said.

That's what he was afraid of. He didn't want Kiki talking about him to Olive at all. What if Kiki said something that made Olive connect him to the guy he'd been in college? But on the other hand, he didn't really have time to debate this with her. "Just be professional."

"Seriously, boss. I always am. I shouldn't have joked around like that. Good luck at the meeting with Brewing Energy Worldwide."

"Thanks. I can't believe he came to us," Dante said.

"I can. He's not stupid."

He just shook his head as Kiki walked away. He went back over to Jeff and they went to lunch.

Three hours later, he was back in the tent, happy with the deal he'd negotiated with Brewing Energy Worldwide. He had dreamed of getting his beer into the European markets but had never imagined it would happen at a beer fest. Now he had a foot in the door.

The tent was busy and he made his way through it, surprised to find Olive back working at the kids' section. She was laughing and talking with the different families who came through, and once again he was struck by the woman she was.

He wanted her. But it was more than just lust. It was her intelligence and her laughter, and as much as it surprised him to say it, her kindness. The Olive who was standing before him today hardly resembled the mean girl he'd first crushed on.

Dante would even say she was prettier now. She had lost that hard outer shell she used to project and he wanted her more now than he had during those long college months when he'd become obsessed with her.

Just thinking of that obsession made him turn away from her and walk out of the tent. Back then, he'd been fooled by the smiles she'd used to get what she wanted. He'd been fooled because he'd been so unsure of himself he hadn't been able to see she'd been a user. But he wasn't that boy anymore and the man he was today had confidence in spades. Her smiles were different now. *She* was different.

It was hot as the sun, but he barely noticed the heat. Was he once again obsessed with her?

This new version of the same woman? The woman he'd somehow always placed just beyond his reach?

He couldn't let that happen again. In fact, the more he thought about it, the more important it seemed to him to stay the path and keep things just professional between them for now. He needed to truly know her so that he didn't do what he had in college. Idolize a woman he hadn't known.

Sure, it was easy to convince himself he saw changes in her when he wanted to sleep with her. But for his peace of mind and long-term happiness, he had to be sure.

"Dante? How'd your meeting go?"

*Olive.*

He turned and smiled at her. "Really good. I'm sorry I had to bail on our lunch. Do you have time to go over the notes you wanted to give me?"

"I do. Let's go find a quiet place to chat," she said. "Kiki gave me a few more notes and we revised the message we want you to deliver."

"I know a quiet place," he told her. The VIP sponsors' tent, where he'd just left his meeting with Jeff. He led Olive over there. Reminded himself he was all business even though he couldn't tear his eyes off her long, sexy legs as she walked in front of him and took a seat at the high tables near the back.

# Eight

Olive was surprised when Dante led her to the quiet area off to the left of the stage as the music started. He'd wowed the crowd and, more and more, she was beginning to believe he hadn't really needed her services at all. There was a natural charm and confidence to him that she'd done nothing to draw out.

Usually when she did a makeover for a client, it was more of "drawing them out of their shell," but there had been none of that with Dante. Not really.

The area was a three-walled structure with fairy lights on the outside of it. There was a small table and two chairs set up with an ice bucket on a pedestal filled with Inferno Brewing Second Circle bottles.

They had a good view of the stage, but it was almost like they were at a private concert as there were high box hedges blocking them from the rest of the crowd.

She'd changed into a sundress as the sun set and Dante was wearing a vintage tee that advertised the band he'd introduced and a pair of designer leather pants that hugged him in all the right spots. As they sat down, he poured her a beer in the engraved Inferno Brewing pint glass.

"This is nice. Finally we can relax," he said. The band was loud, but where they were it wasn't at the ear-shattering decibels she remembered from concerts in her teens and early twenties.

"Yes, *finally*! Tell me something…" she began, waiting until he'd poured his own pint glass and toasted her.

"What?"

"Why did you hire me?" she asked.

"I didn't," he said, wriggling his eyebrows at her. "Kiki did."

"You know what I mean. You could have gotten a haircut and done this on your own. You might have been a bit unkempt, but you didn't really need a 'make-over.'"

He shrugged, took a long swallow of his beer and set his glass on the table. She wondered if he was going to answer her.

"That answer is complicated," he said.

That made sense. There was so much more to

Dante than met the eye. She could tell, by the way he held himself, that he was like a still pond with so much activity going on below the surface. Sighing, she heard the band singing about falling in love on a summer's night, and there were answering butterflies in the pit of her stomach.

Was she falling in love?

No.

*Of course not.*

She wasn't the kind of woman who fell. She made strategic partnerships. But as Dante sang along with the band and then looked over at her and winked, a part of her wanted to be that kind of girl. The kind that a man saw on a summer night and fell for.

She knew she was too scarred. Too deeply broken to be that woman. She was making repairs, but they didn't happen easily or quickly.

"Complicated…just like you?"

"I suppose." He nodded. "I mean, what man wants to think he's simple? Dance with me, Olive."

He held his hand out and she took it. Her pulse skittered as he pulled her close, the two of them moving slowly to the beat, and she couldn't help feeling like this wasn't happening to her. It would be easier if she'd been able to make herself over all those years ago. Throw out old Olive and make some new woman without all the past mistakes.

The song ended and they clapped and then sat back down.

"So you're not simple, which I totally knew," she said, realizing she didn't want to let this go. She wanted to know…well, *everything* about Dante. "We've got all night."

"We do. Maybe I'll tell you later."

She reached over and put her hand on his wrist above his watch, where she noticed he had a knotted leather bracelet that said Be True.

"You can trust me."

"Can I?" he asked thickly. "Right now you and I are sort of stumbling around with attraction and a business relationship, but trust…that's something that is usually reserved for intimates."

*Intimates*. The word hovered in the air between them and she knew what he meant. Olive was asking him to go beyond the boundaries they'd set. She wanted to know more about him. Needed to know more about this man she was trying to deny was more than just some hot guy.

She needed to know the real Dante Russo so she wasn't stuck seeing him only as the man she'd helped make. But had she? That was what she was trying to figure out.

"I could share something personal too, if that's what you are worried about," she said. Surprising even herself. But if she was going to figure out what was going on with the two of them, she was going to have to peel back some of those layers she'd let scab over long ago. She knew it might hurt, but a part of her felt like Dante was worth the risk.

"Really? Like what? You seem pretty fabulous, not like you're hiding anything."

"Do I?" she asked. Sort of glad to hear it but not sure she believed him.

"Yup. What secrets do you have?"

Olive took a deep breath and then a long swallow of her drink. She looked over at him, into those mesmerizing green eyes of his, and for the briefest of moments, had a feeling of déjà vu. Like she'd been close to him before this. Of course, she'd kissed him, so that must be it.

She had to get this off her chest. Had to own her past so she could test the waters with Dante. She didn't know if she'd ever be the kind of woman who fell in love on a summer's night, but she knew until she unburdened the past she never would be.

"I used to be a mean girl. I probably would never have gotten to know you in the past because I would have looked at your shaggy hair and beard and dismissed you as not good enough for me."

Dante just stared at her as the words he was pretty sure he'd never hear from her came out of her mouth. What did he do? It was okay to ignore their past when she hadn't acknowledged it. But now…did he tell her that he knew her?

"I've shocked you, right? Or disappointed you?"

she asked. "Believe me, I'm not proud of it. I got a misdemeanor charge for bullying and had to do three hundred hours of community service. I'd like to say that made me wise up, but I think for the first hundred and fifty hours I felt like I was the victim, and then... well, someone who is now one of my best friends pointed out that I was being a brat and told me to snap out of it."

"Wow," he said, his mind still frantically trying to work out what to say. She'd been more honest than he'd expected her to be and she'd revealed something that should make it easier for him to trust her. Now, if he kept the past to himself, he would be the one lying to her.

Something that he just wouldn't allow himself to do.

"I'm not disappointed," he assured her. "In fact, I think it's incredibly brave of you to open yourself up to me this way."

"I don't know about brave," she divulged. "I sometimes hate the girl I was. But my therapist is adamant that I have to own that. Acknowledge that I'm not her anymore. That's harder than it sounds."

He reached over and took her hand in his, rubbing his thumb across her knuckles. He'd never thought he'd feel sympathy for Olive Hayes, but he did. She was so right when she said it was hard to move on from the past. There were so many times when, despite the fact that he'd started making healthy choices and really taken control of his life, he still felt like that tubby nerd. Not worth anyone's time or attention.

"I was a fat kid," he confessed. "I mean, I didn't feel like there was anything wrong with it. I just had unhealthy habits thanks to a mom who adored... well, still adores me, and thinks I'm the most beautiful human on the planet. Seriously, she still calls me that." He cleared his throat. "Anyway, I was just living my best junk-food-eating, video-game-playing life until I had a wake-up call in college."

"Your mom's not wrong," she said, turning to face him, but there was still so much vulnerability on her face that he almost wondered if she was even hearing anything he was saying. "I think I would have spoiled you too."

He smiled as he knew she intended him to. But she couldn't know what that kind of adoration did to a kid...well, to him. It had made him feel invincible and college had been a rude awakening. He'd done good. Had a great roommate—Max. And the two of them had just done their drinking, eating and partying thing. They'd had each other's backs, and until that moment when Olive had described him at the frat dance, called out his unkempt, soft body, his beard and crazy hair, he hadn't realized that people saw him the way she had.

She'd forced him to see a version of himself he guessed had always been there but he'd never noticed.

"A girl—the one who said I had a weak chin—

pointed out that I wasn't the most beautiful human on the planet. In fact, she thought I wasn't worthy to even be in the same room and speak to her."

"What a bitch! Honestly, I was like that too. Just didn't care about anyone else's feelings. Like I was somehow better," Olive said. "I bet there are tons of people who have stories like that about me."

He started to say it *was* her, but he couldn't bring himself to speak the words. He'd never heard Olive talk this way about herself before. There was an element of self-derision in her voice and he realized, as much as he'd hated her when she'd rejected him so publicly, he'd never wanted this woman to hate herself.

"You were young."

"Perhaps. But you were young too," she said hoarsely. "You shouldn't have been treated that way. I know there's no way that this can make up for it, but I'm sorry for what you went through."

He felt a lump in his throat. She was looking up at him with those big brown eyes and offering a sincere apology to him. He was never going to be able to see that mean girl she'd been when he looked at her again. She'd apologized to him. He'd told her about the moment she'd humiliated him and she hadn't recognized him.

"It does," he said. "I accept your apology. I'd be glad if we could both move on from our pasts."

"Me too." Her mouth tilted up into a half smile.

"Wow, that wasn't what I was expecting to talk about, but honestly, I feel freer having told you. I was afraid you'd be disgusted by me."

Now that they'd both stripped their souls bare, he was ready to put that chapter of his past with Olive behind him. There was no need to tell her she was the girl who'd humiliated him. Not now. They'd both acknowledged who they were and had moved on.

He twined their fingers together, stood and pulled her to her feet, then tugged her into his arms and hugged her close. "I feel lighter too. I'm glad you trusted me enough to tell me."

"Me too," she whispered, resting her head on his shoulder. "I know we said we'd keep this professional but... I'm starting to wish I hadn't suggested that."

Dante looked down into her heart-shaped face, seeing the regrettable parts of her past with the reconciliation she was trying to find in her present. And at this moment he wanted her more than he'd ever wanted anything. He lowered his head and their lips brushed as they swayed to the music. Deepening the kiss, he splayed his hands on her butt and pulled her fully into his body. She wound her arms around his waist, tangling her tongue with his, and when she finally broke the lip-lock, she rested her head on his chest, right over his heart.

And that was beating loudly as he was trying to figure out what to do next. He had her in his arms and it felt right. Olive Hayes felt right. Something he thought he'd never say. But it was the truth and he couldn't let her go.

She tipped her head back and their eyes met, and his conscience niggled. He'd been wrong before. He *should* still come clean about her being the girl who'd hurt him. Instead he lowered his head and kissed her again.

With his embrace he soothed the past hurt they'd both felt. Her tongue in his mouth moved him out of the past and into the present as his cock hardened. She shifted her legs, rubbed herself against his erection.

Yes.

Except was he letting himself hide in a cloud of lust? Allowing himself to get swept away in the moment to avoid telling her the truth? Yes, that was exactly what he was doing, and no matter how he tried to spin this, he knew she deserved to know who he was. He'd given her some of his honesty. The part that was humiliating. But he knew he owed her the other part. The part that he was reluctant to share because it might change things between them forever.

Tingling with the heat from Dante's heart-stopping kiss, Olive felt a sort of peace she hadn't felt in a long time. She had owned her past, told someone who hadn't known her then, and nothing had gone wrong. She'd done what she'd needed to do. It hadn't imploded on her.

The band started to play one of their rock anthems and she pulled back from Dante, feeling those butterflies again. They had turned into the bubbly kind of joy that she couldn't remember the last time she felt. He started dancing to the music and she did too. It was rollicking and they both seemed to let go of all their worries and inhibitions.

Tonight was theirs. It was *magic*.

The kind of magic that she'd never really understood existed in the world.

She had shown Dante the worst part of herself and he'd accepted her. And Olive knew that she would only do better from here on out. She ignored the fact that she'd had some steps backward recently with her jealousy, assigning it to the fact that she'd been developing feelings for Dante. She liked him. That had to be why she'd allowed jealousy to get the better of her.

She was jumping and spinning to the music along with Dante, then he scooped her up in his arms and threw his head back, singing along at the top of his lungs. She joined in. Just singing and laughing beside this handsome, sexy, incredible man and then… she started crying without realizing it.

This was the breakthrough her therapist had told her would happen one day.

Dante noticed her tears and immediately set her down on her feet. He framed her face with his big hands, his thumbs wiping the tears that were streaming down her face.

"Are you okay?" he asked.

"Yes… I think so." She was embarrassed to be crying, but couldn't stop them. "It's so silly. I don't know where these tears are coming from."

He just hugged her close to him and leaned down to whisper in her ear, "It's okay. Cry. I think you're letting go of the guilt from the past."

Was she?

She hoped so. She knew it was not all of the guilt but even relinquishing part of it would be nice.

She just snuggled closer to Dante and realized his mom had been right to adore this man. He was a good, kind human. The type of person that she wished she had been all of her life. But she was getting there now. One step at a time. Admitting to her past and moving forward.

She pulled back, licking her dry lips then shaking her head. "I'm sorry about that."

"Don't be. Emotions are always okay," he said tenderly.

"Most of the time they make people uncomfortable."

"Yeah, it does, but it's not going to help things for you to keep it inside," he told her. "When I got mad, I used to punch the wall in my bedroom. My dad said it was better to talk and, if that didn't work, then to go in the backyard and scream."

"Good advice. I think most people would be horrified if I screamed."

"It definitely isn't for the faint of heart," he said, chuckling, "but here at the concert...we could both scream our heads off and no one would notice. Want to try it?"

Dante lifted both eyebrows at her and she was charmed by him again. She couldn't resist it. So she held his hand tightly in hers and screamed as loud as she could. It was barely discernible in the noise of the concert crowd.

But she heard his scream.

Olive looked over and saw the way he'd thrown his head back, and she realized those butterflies were more than lust and excitement. She was starting to fall for him. She wasn't sure if she'd made him into her ideal man or anything like that, but she *did* know there was still so much to find out about him. And she was excited by the possibilities. She hadn't ever felt this way before and it did scare her a little, but she shoved that emotion right out of her mind. She was going to enjoy this.

"Not bad. What do you say we get out of here? I booked a hotel for the night, if you're interested in going back there with me," he said. "No pressure. You can say no and I won't be upset."

"I like it. I booked a room too. So we can see which one has the better bed," she murmured, making it clear that she wanted him. She'd never been the type of woman to pretend with a man and she wasn't going to start now.

That was one thing her therapist had said was positive about her past. She'd always been honest in her intimate relationships. "Before things get too hot and heavy… I'm on the pill and healthy."

"Well then," he said. "Not on the pill but healthy. I can use a condom too."

"Thanks. I'd appreciate that."

"No problem. I'm a better-safe-than-sorry kind of guy," he said. "We're just getting to know each other, after all, and don't need to add a further complication."

"Agreed. I drove here," she said. "What hotel are you at? I'll meet you there."

He gave her the name of his hotel. They were staying at the same one, and he walked her to her car, kissing her deeply before she got in and drove out of the parking lot.

He followed behind her and she was very aware of him back there.

She might be glancing in the rearview mirror but for the first time she had the future in her mind. She wasn't seeing anything too extreme and she liked the thought that there was a possibility she was growing into the woman she'd always wanted to be.

# Nine

Dante realized all of those one-night stands he'd had made this part of taking a woman to his room seem normal. The first few times, he'd been awkward as hell. And somehow, with Olive by his side, he'd expected some of that to trickle in. But she just slipped her hand in his as they walked down the hall, looking breathtakingly beautiful and sexy as hell. He didn't bother with pretending he wanted anything but her.

He tapped the key card and opened the door to his suite. As soon as the door closed behind them, he lifted their joined hands to the wall behind her head. Putting his hand on her hip, he leaned down until their foreheads were touching and their eyes met. Her gaze was wide and reassured him that she wanted this as much as he did. He lifted his free hand, rubbing his thumb against her cheek. Trying to hit the brakes and make sure he didn't go too fast. He wanted to savor every moment of this night with her.

But it was hard. Hell, *he* was hard. This was Olive Hayes and he'd already realized she was so much more than that girl he'd wanted but hadn't known. But he still didn't want to fuck this up. He felt her hand between their bodies, slowly stroking her way up his chest, bringing the hem of his T-shirt with her until he felt her cool fingers against the pad of the muscles on his chest.

Damn.

Shivers went down his body and he got even harder at her touch. Screw going slow.

Dante lowered his head, brushing his lips over hers. She groaned and opened her mouth under his, her tongue thrusting into his. He sucked it deeper into his mouth, felt her nails scratching over his chest, moving slowly down his body until she was making tiny circles around his belly button while her tongue made an answering movement against his own.

Double damn.

He swept her off her feet and carried her to the bedroom. Cradling her in his arms, he maneuvered them down onto the king-sized bed. His hand slid down her back, finding the tab to the zipper and lowering it until he could push both hands into the open fabric and feel the smoothness of her skin against him.

Dante skimmed his hands up and down her back, reaching lower to cup her butt and draw her closer to him as he kissed her long and slow and deep. Taking everything he wanted from her and realizing he still wanted more. Needed more from her.

He lifted himself and looked down at her. Aware he was still wearing his T-shirt, he shoved it up under his arms and drew it over his head, tossing it aside. When he glanced back at her, she was watching him.

"Don't stop there."

He flashed her a wicked grin. "You want to see more?"

"You know I do."

She leaned back on her elbows, watching him with raised eyebrows.

He rolled off the bed and to his feet. Took a moment to grab the condoms he kept in his wash bag before he came back to her. He put the condoms on the nightstand and then toed off his shoes.

"You like to be prepared," she remarked.

"Sometimes," he admitted. The condoms were in there…he couldn't say why, only that he'd put them in at the last minute. "Maybe I was already thinking about changing our arrangement."

"No maybe about it from where I'm sitting just enjoying the view."

Dante loved the body that he had today, but he was

honest and seeing her admire him did something to his ego that he couldn't ignore. He brought his hands to the fastening of his jeans and slowly undid it. Her eyes were on that opening and he reached inside to cup himself, realizing he was bigger and harder than he'd been in a while. He shoved his jeans down his legs and stepped out of them. Standing in front of her in just his boxer briefs.

She moved to kneel on the bed, pulled the hem of her sundress up over her head and tossed it aside. He caught his breath at her nakedness. Her tiny waist and her full breasts with beaded nipples beckoned him. In that one move, she'd evened the score. Olive wore only the tiniest pair of black lace bikini panties, but they didn't stay on long, because a moment later she crawled off the bed and shimmied them down her legs. Then, kicking off her sandals, she shot him a hot, sultry look, and his mind deserted his body. He was one big hormone focused only on claiming her.

She shook her head as he took two large steps toward her and held out her hand. "Not until you're naked too."

He shoved his boxer briefs down his legs so fast, he stumbled as he stepped out of them. Then he reached for her, but her hands were there first. Both of them moving all over his torso, caressing every inch of him.

"I can't believe you were hiding this delicious body under that lumberjack chic the day we met," she said.

"Clothes don't define me," he said, not sure really what he was saying because at that moment she was close enough that he could touch her left breast. Cup it in his hand and feel the hardness of her nipple in the center of his palm.

He rotated his hand, feeling her nipple get even harder, and then her fingers were once again moving down his stomach. Only this time she didn't stop at his belly button. She went lower, cupping his balls and then wrapping her hand around his shaft and stroking him from the root to the tip. Her finger swiping over the top of it.

He groaned her name. It sounded rough and guttural. All of the sophistication he'd garnered over the years gone by one touch from Olive.

He pulled her closer, his mouth coming down hard on hers as she stroked his cock and brought him to the very edge of his control. It was the second time she'd done it tonight. The first had been with her honesty.

Olive hadn't expected Dante to look this good under his clothes. He was muscle-bound, lean and athletic. No bodybuilder six-pack, just a really hot guy who didn't have to work at it. And that was turning her on faster than she'd expected.

His erection grew as she stroked him, and his mouth on hers was doing things to her that drove her wild. She felt a throbbing ache deep inside and wanted more from him. And somewhere in the back of her brain a warning tried to sound. Telling her that doing this tonight with him after she'd bared her soul to him might leave her vulnerable.

But she shut that down.

It had been a long time since she'd just felt joy and been happy in the moment, and right now she was, and it was enough. It had to be. She was going to stay present and not worry about anything except how big his dick was and if she was going to be able to take all of him.

She broke the kiss and put her free hand on his chest, urging him back to the bed. He fell backward once he was closer to it and she let go of his dick as he fell. He sprawled his legs wide and scooted back until he was in the center of the mattress.

She climbed onto the bed, sitting on her knees between his spread legs. She looked up his body, at his erection, and licked her lips. He was on his elbows, watching her as she took her time examining him. She noticed he had a jagged scar on his knee and ran her fingers over it. It had healed a long time ago. She moved her touch further up his thigh, on the inside, unable to resist touching his cock again.

He rocked his hips as she closed her hand around his shaft and shut his eyes, moaning as he did so. She worked with her hand and then leaned forward to take him in her mouth. He tasted so good and she took him as deeply as she could. She felt his hand on the back of her head in her hair, stroking her. Olive reached under him to stroke his balls and she felt his hips thrust again. He pulled her off his cock, sitting up and lifting her to straddle him.

His big hands were on her back and then his lips were on her breast, sucking her nipple deep into his mouth. She rocked against his shaft and put her hands on his shoulders. He was so strong. She never would have guessed at the strength in him when she first saw him.

He'd been this big teddy bear, but she noticed now that he'd been hiding his strength. Keeping it safely tucked away. She wondered why for a moment but then the thought was gone as the aching want inside her grew, demanding her attention. She shifted until she felt the tip of him at her entrance, but he pulled back. His mouth leaving her breast as he leaned toward the nightstand.

The condom.

Olive left his lap and crawled to the head of the bed to get it. She felt his hand on her butt. Cupping one cheek and then his fingers lightly feathering between them. She glanced back over her shoulder at him, and he was watching her body. Seeming entranced by it. His other hand was on the back of her thigh, moving toward her pussy. She grabbed the box of condoms and fumbled to open it, taking one out, holding it in a tight grip in her hand.

She stayed on her hands and knees and felt him moving up behind her. His cock rubbed against her butt and his chest against her back. He braced himself with one hand and the other cupped her breast as his mouth was on the back of her neck, hotly kissing her. He teased her nipple with his fingers as his mouth moved down her spine. She shivered and arched her back into his touch. Wanting and needing so much more from him.

She reached between them, catching the edge of his cock, but he pulled his hips back from her touch. "No."

"Why?" It was all she could force herself to say since her mind and body were on fire for him.

"I'm going to come if you touch me again."

Those words made her shiver and she realized how close to the edge she was. She turned to face him. They were both kneeling as she opened the condom and put it on him. "I don't want to wait any longer."

He groaned.

"Me either, but I also don't want it to end."

"Who says we can only do it once?"

His hips jerked toward her and she nudged him backward until he was seated and she could straddle him again. She shifted her center until she felt the tip of him poised at her entrance, and their eyes met.

Something passed between them. Probably the truth of that shared but different past they had. The fact that somehow they'd both survived and thrived and were now here together. She kissed him as deeply as she could as she slowly lowered herself on his shaft.

Damn.

He was a tight fit, but she kept going until she'd taken him all in. She waited once he was inside her, giving her body a moment to adjust. Then she felt Dante's hands roaming down her back, cupping her butt and lifting her slightly, urging her to ride him.

She let her head fall back as she did. Just took him again and again, driving herself toward an orgasm and letting everything else fall away.

Dante felt her driving harder and faster against him, and then her body tightened around his cock and he grabbed her butt to take control of her thrusts, relentless until she called his name. Then, spent, she collapsed against him, her head on his shoulder as he kept driving until he felt his own orgasm rush through him. He kept thrusting until he was empty, and then fell to his side, cradling her in his arms as he disengaged their bodies.

She nestled her head on his chest, had one leg over the top of his thighs, and he had his arms around her, holding her to him. He stroked her back, trying to catch his breath and waiting to feel normal again.

Except he wasn't going to feel normal again. There was no way. This was something he'd wanted for a long time and then had vowed would never happen, and here he was...in bed with Olive Hayes.

Except she was just Olive. Right now as she tipped her head back and smiled up at him. He couldn't connect this woman with the heartless one who'd made him think that he could have any kind of sexual revenge on her.

He knew he was going to have to unpack this, but later. Not now. Right now, he wanted to hold her and talk to her. Like they were just a normal couple. Not one with a complex past that only one of them was aware of.

He sighed.

"What?"

He couldn't do it. Couldn't tell her the truth that was now sticking in his stomach like a large piece of lead. "Condom's starting to feel gross… I'll be right back."

He got off the bed and went into the bathroom, closing the door behind him. He tossed the used condom in the trash can and braced his hands on the countertop, not able to look at himself in the mirror.

A part of him—the biggest part of him—wanted to just go back out there and enjoy the rest of this night with Olive. Just pretend she was an image consultant he'd met at work and they were starting to like each other.

But another part knew they weren't that. And damn it all, he wished he could be that guy he'd always thought he was. The careless serial dater just in it for a good time. But he wasn't. He'd never been in the past and he certainly wasn't now with her.

He was going to have to tell her the truth.

But maybe…could he have this one night? He'd come clean in the morning and then see what happened. He finished cleaning up and went back into the room to find Olive wearing his T-shirt and sitting at the top of the bed. She had a variety of drinks and snacks spread out in front of her.

"I hope you don't mind, but I raided the minibar."

"I don't." He quirked a brow. "What have you got?"

"Peanut M&M's, my fav. I wasn't sure what you liked so just grabbed everything else. You know I don't normally like peanuts at all but can't resist them in an M&M," she said.

He realized she was sort of manically talking about snacks and she hadn't really looked at him since he'd come back into the room. He pulled on his boxer briefs and then walked over to sit next to her on the bed.

"What's up?"

"Why does something have to be up?" she countered.

He put his hand under her chin and turned her face toward him. "You're not acting like you. Second thoughts?"

She shook her head. "Never."

"I'm glad to hear that. So, what then?"

She took a deep breath and held it for a few seconds before exhaling on a long breath. "Um. I've never told anyone I've dated about my past. And so, I guess I'm feeling more…unsure than I normally would be after sex."

He shifted until he was leaning back against the headboard and then pulled her into his arms so she was nestled against the side of his body.

"And I've never told anyone that I slept with that I used to be fat and a girl publicly rejected me," he admitted.

She turned and put her hand on his jaw. "That girl was a loser."

"Maybe," he said carefully. He had to tell her the truth but he didn't want to ruin this. "Or maybe she was a stranger, and I should have tried to get to know her first."

"She probably didn't want to know you," Olive said. "I hate that I was ever that way."

"But you learned from it and are a better person now," he said. Really starting to believe she had. He'd seen her with her staff, with his employees, and even with the general public today. The Olive he was holding wasn't the same woman she used to be. "Don't regret anything about this night."

"You know the funny thing is that I don't. I'm glad to have finally told someone…glad that it was you," she said softly.

"I'm glad too."

She smiled and then kissed him. "So TV and

snacks? I can't just go to sleep or do it again this quickly."

"TV sounds good. I think there's a game on—"

"No way. I think there's a new rom-com on that I want to watch. A guy has been on a thousand first dates and can't find love," she said.

"Sounds like he's a loser," Dante grumbled.

She lightly punched him on the shoulder. "Rock, paper, scissors to choose."

Charmed, despite himself, he nodded. She was something unexpected…and he couldn't help it. He was starting to fall for her, as ill-advised as it might be, given their past and the fact that he hadn't told her who she was to him.

They rock, paper, scissored, and both did rock the first time. That made her laugh. He hadn't realized how much he could adore a person's laugh until that moment.

They did it again and he beat her with paper.

"Fair's fair," she said, not sulking at losing. She made sure they both had snacks and cuddled next to him to watch the game.

Dante didn't know how, but the woman who'd broken him felt so right in his arms. She did. And he realized how much he didn't want to let her go.

# Ten

Tuesday nights weren't normally for late-night gab sessions but Delaney had gotten Stanley back and they all wanted to see her sweet dog. So Paisley had suggested a sleepover. Since her Wednesday was light with morning meetings, Olive had said yes. She was bringing a six-pack of Inferno's Second Circle beer, the makings of her daddy's famous shrimp tacos and, of course, her secret of having slept with Dante.

Delaney's condo overlooked Lake Michigan and had a patio that stretched the entire length of it. She had spared no expense when purchasing her place, so the patio had one of those huge built-in grills with a pizza oven, a beverage fridge and a fully stocked bar. The seating was these super-comfy, large padded chairs that flanked a three-seater couch. There was also a firepit so when the sun set they wouldn't get cold.

Olive had been greeted by Stanley, who'd immediately gone back to Delaney and kept licking her friend's hand. It seemed her dog had missed her as much as she had missed him. Paisley was dropped off by Jack, and both she and Delaney stood in the front window and watched him kiss her goodbye.

"She's a goner. When is she going to admit he's the one?" Delaney asked.

"Never. Because she swore after everything she saw in her parents' marriage she'd never let herself be that vulnerable." Olive rolled her eyes. "You know how she is. She's probably trying to find a flaw in a man that anyone else would be trying to get to the altar as fast as they could."

The doorbell rang and Delaney and Stanley went to let Paisley in. Olive went into the kitchen to check on the shrimp she'd set in a marinade when she'd arrived.

"Hiya," Paisley said when she came in. "I'm so glad we are doing this. We've been too busy lately."

"Agreed. I mean, you two at least like working but, for me, it's like, ugh!" Delaney said. "I sort of didn't mind doing that job with Keats because he's one of my fav cousins, but lately it's all work."

"Dellie, stop. You know you like your clients," Olive admonished.

"I do. But I like me more," Delaney said with a laugh.

"So what are we drinking?"

"I brought some of Dante's beer if you want to try it," Olive said.

"Love to. Actually I'm really into Seventh Circle," Paisley said. "I know that's anger, but it's spicy and I like it."

"No comment," Olive said. "I brought Second Circle."

"Of course you did," Delaney said. "You are into someone."

"Am I?" Olive demurred. Not sure yet if she was going to divulge everything that had happened with Dante.

"Yes, you are," Paisley said. "We both know it. So who *is* this mystery man?"

Delaney got chilled beers from her fridge and poured them all a glass, which the other women carried to the patio while Olive brought the shrimp and the taco fixings.

"It's Dante," she finally divulged.

"I'm not surprised," Paisley said. "He must be into you to pick you up and take you to the suburbs."

"He did that? When?" Delaney asked. "Oh, was it that night I went home with Raul?"

"You went home with *Steve* the night that Dante gave me a lift," Olive reminded her. "We have been trying to keep things platonic while we are still

working together, but last weekend in Milwaukee...
things heated up."

"Oooh, that sounds fun. What were you doing in
Milwaukee?" Delaney asked.

"I'm happy for you, but you need to be careful
since you're now sleeping with a client," Paisley in-
terjected.

"Did I say I slept with him?" Olive asked. Damn.
She should have stuck to the original arrangement
they'd made. She didn't want to cause any problems
for their company.

"You didn't have to," Paisley said. "It's okay. I
mean, I'm sure you two discussed it."

"God, I hope you didn't," Delaney huffed. "What
a buzzkill that would be. Hey, can you sign this HR
waiver before we get busy?"

Olive shook her head and took the shrimp off the
grill, setting it on the serving counter. "It wasn't like
that. I mean, we had both discussed not doing anything intimate until we were done working together
but things just sort of progressed—"

"You don't have to justify it," Delaney said. "Paisley and I have your back."

"We do. Just be careful," Paisley cautioned her.
"So how was it?"

"Great," Olive said. "I mean... I told him about
my past and he was cool with it. It was the first time
I felt like I was sleeping with a guy who knew who I
really was."

They took their food to the seating area and the three of them sat down. "I wasn't sure how he'd react, but I think I need to stop keeping it hidden. It's like I'm ashamed, and, deep down, I guess I still am, but I can't be ashamed forever."

Paisley one-arm hugged her and Delaney winked at her.

"It's about time you figured that out," Delaney said.

"I'm happy about this. Dante sounds like a great guy." Paisley arched a brow. "So what's next?"

"I don't know," Olive confessed. "I mean, we both had our own cars and he had promised his staff to do team building at the Mars Cheese Castle in Kenosha, so I came home… Yesterday we texted some, but as for where we stand, I don't know."

That was the truth. She had typed and deleted about a dozen different versions of "So do you want to hang out or are we dating now?" But he hadn't sent her a message except to make sure she'd gotten home safely and to let her know he was back in town. That was it. So she was in a holding pattern and had no real idea how to get out of it.

"Give it time," Paisley advised her.

"I am," Olive said. "But enough about me. What's with you and Jack?"

Paisley sighed. "I don't know. He's great. He moved in with me and we really get along. I mean, he's not messy, he brings me coffee in bed and puts the toilet seat down."

"All the important things. So what don't you know?" Delaney asked.

"I'm not sure. It could be just me hesitating like I do or something else. My gut just doesn't know yet," Paisley said.

"I don't know about men either," Delaney admitted. "Stanley is the only man I'm going to fall in love with."

*"Tonight,"* Olive and Paisley said together.

The three of them started laughing and some of the tension that Olive had been carrying around since she'd gotten back to Chicago disappeared. She'd figure this thing with Dante out and, no matter what happened, at least she had her two besties by her side.

Max showed up in his office on Tuesday evening with baby Rosie in her carrier and takeaway wings from their favorite pub. He plopped the baby, who was sleeping, on Dante's desk.

"Since you didn't come to me, I had to haul myself and my baby girl all the way into the city during rush hour."

"You were going the opposite direction of most of the traffic and I told you I'm busy," Dante said. "But it's good to see you."

He walked around his desk and gave his friend a bro hug before going to the fridge and grabbing a couple of beers for them. "What is it that couldn't wait?"

"Nothing. Mia's having a trunk show at our house tonight and the last time, her and her friends were so loud, I couldn't hear the game, so I figured I'd just get out of the house."

"What in the hell is a trunk show?"

"I'll be honest, dude, I'm not sure. But it involves people coming to our house and buying stuff," he said. "Rosie and me figured we come see her favorite uncle."

Since Rosie was sleeping and it was a weekday, he was starting to get concerned that Max might be here for more than just an escape. "Everything okay with you and Mia?"

"What? Yeah, why'd you think that?" he asked warily.

"Because you're acting weird."

He grimaced and then took a long swallow of his beer before he put it down, shoving his hand through his hair. "I hate my job. I almost quit today and I can't. I mean, I have financial obligations and Mia shouldn't be expected to support us, but honestly I don't know how much longer I can do this."

Dante felt for Max. It had been a total accident, but Dante had found a career he liked. He sat down next to his friend. "Want to be legal counsel for me? Inferno Brewing is getting bigger and I could use someone I can trust."

Max turned and stared at him. Dante wondered

if he'd overstepped, but this was his best friend, and
the only reason he hadn't gone to him sooner was
that Dante had thought he was happy where he was.

"Seriously? Or is this a pity thing?"

"Seriously. I trust you more than anyone else I'd
hire," Dante told him. "We're doing a deal to distribute
in Europe and I'm not sure our legal guy can handle
it. I'd love to have you work for Inferno, and you've
been saying for years I should have my own legal department."

"Let me talk to Mia… I mean, yes, of course, but
we promised each other we'd discuss all big decisions, so I can't do this until…thanks, dude," he said.

"You're welcome. You're doing me a favor."

"I'm not, but it's nice of you to make it seem like
I am. When do you need me to start?" Max asked.

"Tonight," he said. "*Joking*. But as soon as you
can."

"Are you sure you want to bring me on board?"
Max asked.

Dante nodded. This man had saved his sanity
more times than he could count and having his friend
work with him was about the best idea he'd ever had.
"Yes. A hundred percent."

They ate the wings and baby Rosie woke up. Dante
held his goddaughter and walked her around the office while Max cleaned up. When his friend came
back, they settled on the couch in his private confer-

ence room, watching the skyline of the city through the floor-to-ceiling windows.

"How's it going with Olive?" Max asked.

*Olive.*

He'd been unsure if he should just let one time be enough until he told her that he'd known her in college. He had to tell her, and right now he was letting his hectic work schedule be the reason he wasn't texting her.

"Dan?"

"We slept together."

"Oh-ho. So is it...?"

*Is it what?* he thought. But he knew what Max was asking. "Not revenge sex. I mean, she's not even the Olive Hayes we knew in college. She's so different now. Soft and sweet and so open about things. She told me she was a 'classic mean girl.'"

"Did you say 'yeah, I know'?"

"Uh, not exactly," Dante said.

"What *did* you say then?"

This was complicated and talking to Max was making him face the harsh reality of what he probably should have said. "We were talking in general terms and I mentioned someone had sort of been a mean bully to me in college, and she said she'd been that girl. Then she apologized for the girl who bullied me and I... I just couldn't tell her it was her."

Max looked at him incredulously. Even baby

Rosie made a sort of questioning sound. He felt judged. He needed to own this.

"I'm going to tell her."

"I know you will. And soon…don't wait too long. But, Dante, it's not going to be easy."

Dante looked at his friend and knew he was right. It wasn't easy keeping this from Olive. And yet telling her was going to be the hardest thing he'd ever had to do.

After Max had gone home, Dante decided to text Olive, but he wasn't sure what to say. He had his feet on the table in front of him, still staring out at the city, and was holding his phone loosely in his hands. He had the classics station on in the background and when they cut to the commercials, he heard his own voice.

"Summer is the season with endless days and endless possibilities. A time for taking chances and making promises. Owning your vices and learning to live with them. Whichever circle appeals to you, know that there is a way out of it. The Inferno is just one part of your life, not the entire thing."

He stopped talking and the jingle played. Dante hit the pause button on his phone. Business had always been easier for him than real life. He always saw himself as a go-getter, a confident man who made no mistakes when it came to Inferno Brewing. But in real life, he was the complete opposite of that.

That man was complex, flawed…real.

A man who made mistakes. Like not owning his truth to Olive. Only going halfway. But honestly, he'd never expected her to confess what she had done or to apologize. He felt sort of like he was the bully now. Had he allowed her to make him into one?

Dante sighed. Okay, deep down he knew that wasn't true. He was reaching for straws and some way to justify his behavior as if what he'd done could be justified in any way.

To be honest, he had no idea where she was. She hadn't exactly been blowing up his phone trying to get in touch with him since they'd both been home. Maybe it was going to turn out to be a one-night thing after all.

He scratched the back of his neck. He needed to get out of his head.

"Boss, what are you still doing here?" Kiki asked from the doorway.

"What are *you* doing here?" he countered, glancing at his watch. It was almost eleven. She should have gone home hours ago.

"I picked up a creeper at the bar and didn't want to order an Uber home in case he followed me. So I came here. Figured I'd hang out for a while."

He patted the couch next to him. "Hang with me. Then I'll drive you home."

She came and sat next to him. She smelled of tequila and club. Sort of stale smoke and perspiration.

She rested her head on the back of the couch. "What are you doing here?"

"Max came to get away from a trunk show his wife was throwing and we were hanging," he said. "Do you know what a trunk show is?"

"Yeah. It's where a brand does a kind of bespoke sale in someone's home. I wonder what brand it was."

"Max had no clue what it even was," he said.

He let the silence grow between them, not really sure what to say to Kiki. She felt sad to him tonight and he got that. Dating was hard. There was no easy way to meet another person and open yourself up to them and stay safe at the same time. He hated that.

"So the creeper…"

"Ugh! Don't get me started. I've seen him a few times before and he seemed cool, but tonight he was just on the hunt," Kiki said. "I just wasn't into it. I think I'm tired of just sleeping with randos."

"Yeah, I got that way too in my midtwenties. It's fine for a while and then…"

"Just gets stale," she said. "I don't want marriage or anything like that, but a cool guy to hang out with and sleep with, I'd like that."

He realized he wanted that with Olive. "Can I ask you something? You can say no."

"Oh, I'll say no if it's weird," she said.

"It's not. I'm sort of seeing someone—"

"Olive."

"Right… Olive. I haven't really texted her in

twenty-four hours because I don't want to come across like your creeper—"

"Boss, you're in a totally different league, and I've seen Olive with you. There's something between the two of you."

"You think?"

"Yeah, she's into you," Kiki said.

Good to know that Kiki thought so. "Thanks. Ready to go home?"

"Yeah. Remind me on Friday night that I don't want to go to the club again."

"I won't have to," he said. "We have that Brewers Association dinner."

"That's right. Text Olive about that—you can ask her to be your date without it seeming like you're asking her out if you're not sure if she wants to date," Kiki said.

He liked her suggestion. "Do I seem like I'm not sure?"

"Not really. I think you know what you want to do but don't want to push because you work together."

"Exactly."

Kiki changed the subject back to work stuff as they walked to the parking garage.

He drove her home and waited until she got safely inside her apartment building before he started to drive to his place. Kiki's suggestion was a safe way to text Olive. But he'd never been a coward. Even in college he'd been sure of himself.

"Siri, text Olive Hayes."

"What would you like me to say?"

"'Sorry I haven't texted sooner. I really enjoyed our weekend together. Do you want to have dinner this week?' Send."

Siri read his message back to him and then sent it.

Dante felt better having reached out. He needed to see her again and he was going to tell her the truth of their shared past so that they could move forward from it. Because tonight had clarified that he did know what he wanted for his future. His beer empire to keep growing and for Olive to be by his side.

# Eleven

The text from Dante had changed everything, and Olive had gone from not being sure to the confident woman she'd once been. It was tempered with her new perspective on the world and her place in it. But she really liked Dante. There was a part of her that was still unsure, of course, because it was hard to trust her instincts when she'd never really been able to.

As she got out of her Uber in front of the large mansion, which by the way wasn't in the suburb she lived in but on Lake Michigan's most prestigious address, she took a deep breath. She was wearing a mini sundress with a deep vee in the front and the back, and the skirt ended midthigh. Olive had paired the blue floral dress with a pair of wedged heels and was carrying her large workbag as she'd come from the office.

She hit the doorbell and heard it play the jingle for Inferno Brewing. It made her smile because it was so Dante to have it here. He seemed grounded in remembering where his money had come from. The door opened and Dante stood in front of her, wearing a pair of plaid shorts and a blue polo shirt that made his green eyes pop. His feet were bare.

She must have seen men dressed this way all her life and thought it was boring…but *damn*. Dante made everything he wore hot. So much so that she wanted to jump into his arms and plant a long, wet kiss on him.

He smiled when he saw her and stepped back so she could enter. The foyer was cream marble with an inlay in the middle of it that showed the nine circles of hell. She found the wall décor to be tasteful, and there were two large tables on either side. He closed the door behind her and took her bag before putting it on one of the tables.

"Hey. How's it going?"

"Hi. Good," she said. "So this doesn't look like Westmont to me."

Dang it. She was nervous now that she was standing next to him. There was no way to pretend this was normal. It wasn't. He stirred something inside her

Those words sparked something inside her. Dante was a decent man, and the fact that he had told a little white lie to make her feel safer just made her like him even more. She had to admit it was getting harder and harder to find a reason not to let herself care for him.

"Thank you."

He shrugged. "It was nothing. I couldn't have left you there waiting for an Uber, just didn't seem the gentlemanly thing to do. I mean, I know it's not trendy to do that stuff, but that's just me."

"I'm glad. I liked it," she said softly.

She followed him out into his backyard, which had a large outdoor kitchen and eating area that over-looked a huge pool with a waterfall at one end. He cooked their food while they talked about everything and nothing. And her heart started to melt a little bit. Here was the man she'd never thought she'd find for herself. A man who was nice and sexy and normal. And accepted her for exactly who she was.

Her gut was leery of trusting him, and her soul so heavy from the karmic ledger that she was still working to clear wasn't sure either. But even so, as they took their second glass of wine with them and walked through his manicured garden as the lights came on, she knew she was falling for him.

Dante kept looking for an opportunity to tell Olive about their past. That she was the mean girl who'd hurt him. He almost had when she'd said Northwestern. That was the perfect opening. But he'd rationalized it was too early in the evening...then come up with a million other excuses.

Like as soon as he'd seen her standing in his house, he'd realized how much he'd missed her. How was that even possible?

It had only been three days since he'd been with her. But he'd felt a bit lost without her. Then she'd smiled at him and his instincts had sprung to life. Demanding he do everything in his power to keep her here with him, which he knew wasn't good. That meant he already knew that once he told her the truth, she was going to leave. She was going to be mad as hell at him.

Rightly so.

That did nothing to explain why he had said nothing during dinner or when he'd offered to take her on a tour of his garden.

She looked so beautiful during the golden hour as the sun was setting. She had always been the one woman he couldn't take his eyes off, but knowing her now made that ache more keen.

He wanted to touch her as they strolled side by side, but with the secret he had to tell hanging over him, he knew that he couldn't. He could maybe justify sleeping with her once without saying anything, but twice...there was no way.

"This is a really nice place. How long have you wanted a big family?" she asked.

He choked on the sip of wine he'd just taken.

"I'm not asking you to marry me," she said with a note of amusement in her voice. "It seemed like a normal thing to ask."

He nodded. "I haven't thought much about a family. I've been busy making beer and selling it. But yeah, someday, I think I'd like one. What about you?"

She moved closer to the willow trellis that had night-blooming jasmine interwoven with lights. He watched her standing there underneath it, looking like a being from another world, and he wondered how he was ever going to tell her the truth.

Once he did, nothing would be the same between them.

"I don't know," she said. "I have a lot of red in my karmic ledger and I'm working to clear it, but I don't think I should have a family until that's taken care of."

*He. Had. To. Tell. Her.*

Right now.

This woman was really trying to make amends for her past and he had the key to closure for her on one count.

She shrugged and wrinkled her nose at him. "Probably not the answer you were expecting."

"No, it wasn't, but it seems right somehow. I have never met anyone who has owned their past the way you have," he stated gruffly.

She tipped her head to the side and then leaned over to sniff one of the blossoms. "You have."

But he hadn't. Not really. Dante walked over to her and took a moment to realize that once he told her, he was going to have to give her space. He wasn't sure he could do it. Be that selfless. Give up this woman who was somehow everything he would have said he wanted if someone had asked him. Olive fucking Hayes.

He put his hand on her head, let the silky-soft red strands run through his fingers and leaned down to kiss her. She turned and their lips met. That electric tingle shot through him and he wasn't sure he could do it.

He had told himself all the "right" things to do. All the things he should say and the way he should behave, but now that she was here…

He broke the kiss. She looked startled.

"Are you okay?"

"Yeah. I want to show you something," he said. Taking her hand in his, he led her through the willow trellis to the other side, where the garden sloped upward until they were about fifteen feet above it on a patio with a seating area that looked back toward the house over the garden and the pool.

"This is gorgeous," she breathed.

"It's why I bought the house," he said.

"So not just for your parents?"

"No. I mean, I hoped they'd retire and just let me take care of them," he said. "They didn't like that at all."

She laughed. "You really care about people, don't you?"

"No more than others," he said.

"I'm not sure that's true. I saw you with your staff. And how you really know what's going on in their lives. Not everyone is like that."

He tried to be a good man. It wasn't really that hard to stay present and, for the most part, until Olive had come back into his life, he'd known where he was going. But now, confronted with her…everything he'd thought he'd known about himself had been thrown into a complete tailspin.

"Well, thanks… I guess. But I'm not always self-less."

"Really?" she asked, crossing her arms beneath her breasts and looking up at him from under eyelashes.

He decided then that he wasn't going to tell her the truth tonight. That he didn't want anything to ruin this night.

Dante knew that wasn't a good enough reason but he didn't care. He wanted this. He wanted a perfect night with Olive in this house that he had bought for his future family. And, for some reason, the only woman he could see with him was standing beside him right now.

He knew that wasn't going to happen. That once she knew the truth, she'd be out the door and then out of his life. That she'd look at her karmic ledger and maybe think she'd erased some of the debt there. But she'd never forgive him, and he wouldn't blame her.

He was going to hurt her the way she had hurt him even though that hadn't been his intention.

It started raining, cold and surprising. Olive yelped and Dante grabbed her hand, leading her to the pool house. They stood under the cover of the overhang. She turned to look up at him. His thick curly hair clung to his head and his green eyes were troubled. She could tell he had something on his mind and she guessed it was more than this casual evening had netted.

He started to speak but she went up on her tiptoes and kissed him. That one kiss under the trellis hadn't been enough. She'd missed him. Missed the feel of his body against her and his mouth moving over hers.

He took control of the kiss, wrapping his arms around her and pulling her fully into his body.

She shivered but knew that was from his mouth on hers and not the air. She had wanted him since she'd left him in Milwaukee.

He lifted his head, looked down into her eyes with an intensity that almost frightened her. "I don't have a condom."

"It's okay. I'm on the pill, remember?"

Her wet clothes clung to her body. The dress she wore was damp. She shuddered as he pulled her back against his body. Olive felt his erection as he rubbed it against her butt, and glanced over her shoulder at him. But he didn't say anything. She lowered his head and bit the side of his neck.

She turned in his arms, shoving his shirt up so she could push her hands underneath the fabric. He was warm and the hair on his chest abraded her fingers as she stroked her hands over him.

She swallowed hard as he found her nipples through the fabric of her dress and tweaked them. Olive was aching and needed him inside of her again. He led her to the lounger on the porch and sat down, then drew her left leg up on the bench near his hips. She straddled him, threading her hands through his hair as she found his mouth.

Thrusting her tongue deep into his mouth, she rocked against his cock. She reached between their bodies and found his hands there. He pushed his hand into her panties, and his fingers separated her until he was rubbing her clit.

The scent of his expensive cologne and the summer rain and the flowers were all around her and she felt transported out of her life. Out of the mistakes she'd made in the past. This felt like a step toward a future she'd never allowed herself to want.

Olive arched against him, ripping her mouth from his. God, she'd never wanted anything as much as she wanted him inside her. Now.

Finding the zipper on his shorts, she undid it, reaching inside his pants to stroke the ridge of his cock until he groaned and pulled away from her so he could free himself from his briefs.

"Take your panties off," he commanded.

She didn't hesitate and stood up to take them off. Glancing over at him, she noticed he was watching her. She lifted the skirt of her dress, and the realization that he was staring at her exposed body with heated desire in his eyes emboldened her even more. She hiked the skirt up further and he groaned again.

Power coursed through her as she took another step closer to him. Olive let the hem of her dress fall back into place and he murmured an objection, but she turned and bent over to undo the strap of her sandal.

She felt the brush of his fingers against the back of her thigh, and then he pushed her dress up to her hips. The feel of his fingers on her skin made her tremble and she was so swept up in the moment she wasn't sure she was going to be able to get her shoes off. But then it didn't matter because she felt his mouth on her, moving from her back to her side, his hands urging her to turn for him. She did and then she closed her eyes as he parted her gently. He tickled her clit with his tongue and then pushed one finger up inside her. Her knees buckled and she braced herself with her hands on his shoulders. He kept his mouth moving over her as his finger thrust in and out of her body until she arched in his arms and cried his name as her orgasm washed over her.

He shifted under her as she sank down on his lap. His cock slid inside her and she moaned again. He clutched her buttocks with his hands, drove himself up into her harder and harder until she was shaking and desperate for another climax. He thrust up into her one more time as he spilled himself inside her. She held him until he was spent and then both stared into each other's eyes.

"I…" *Love you*, she thought. But something stopped her from saying it.

"I have something to tell you, Olive."

"What is it?" she asked. Not sure what it could be, there was a gravity in his voice that warned her it wasn't going to be more about his favorite foods or movies. "Should we get dressed before you tell me?"

"Sorry, I didn't mean to blurt it out like that. Let's go up to the house and talk," he said.

"Okay," she said, turning away to search for her panties. His hand appeared with them and she took them with a murmured thanks.

"I really like you and don't want to screw this up," he said at last.

She nodded. "I like you too, Dante."

He opened his arms and she stepped into him. He hugged her as if he never wanted to let her go, and she felt as if maybe whatever it was might just be something hard for him to say. Nothing too bad.

But there was a lump in her stomach that she couldn't quite ignore as they walked back to his house.

# Twelve

*I went to Northwestern. I was one of the people you publicly humiliated...* He just said those words in his head over and over as they walked back to the house. Olive had to use the bathroom and had taken her bag in with her. He washed up in a guest bathroom and put on jeans and a button-down before heading for the living room to wait for her.

He shoved his hands through his hair and then realized that this cut Pietro had given him was pretty much everything proof as it fell back into place, and he caught a glimpse of himself in the mirror in the hallway.

As he saw his reflection, he realized that if he'd

looked like this in college, Olive wouldn't have treated him the way she had. What did that mean?

He leaned to look into his eyes. As usual, they looked the same as they always did except when he was hungover. Fuck him. He didn't have to feel bad that he'd slept with her again and not told her. He just didn't.

It wasn't like she slept with schlubby him and suddenly "liked him." She liked him because he looked like he fit in with her crowd. And he knew he was being unfair, but he felt cornered by his own silence. He tried to mess his hair up but it just fell back into place.

Hell.

Dante noticed the powder room door was directly behind him. He knew he was feeling anxious but couldn't just stand in the hallway waiting for her. Cursing under his breath, he turned away and strode into the kitchen. He started to pour himself another glass of wine, but he didn't want it. Instead, he got a glass of cold water.

His phone buzzed and he glanced down to see a news alert. Kiki had set up notifications for the company, so he expected it to be about beer fest, but instead he frowned as he read that the local soap heiress had been arrested for trespassing.

Dish soap heiress…wasn't that Olive's friend?

He went to the hallway again and knocked on the door.

"Yes?"

"Uh, I think your friend is in trouble," he said.

The door opened and it looked like she'd been crying. *Fuck.* He'd done this. There was no way to make this right.

"Which one?"

"Dish soap heiress," he said. "Sorry, they didn't list her name."

"Delaney. Can I see your phone?" she asked frantically.

He handed it to her and she skimmed it. Her hands were shaking, and she gave him back his phone before reaching into the powder room. He could hear her fumbling for her phone. She took it out.

"Is there anything I can do to help?" he asked.

"I'm not sure yet," she said. He put his hand on her shoulder and squeezed.

She got her bag and walked to the kitchen while texting.

She waited and he watched her. She had put on a headband and, other than her red eyes, she looked normal. But he'd been with enough women to know he'd screwed up. He could have timed his *we have to talk* better. He knew that. But the problem was that keeping quiet was eating at him. Making him feel like he was turning into the very thing he didn't want to be.

An arrogant asshole who thought no one was as important as he was.

"Damn. Paisley doesn't know what's going on,

either, and Delaney isn't answering. Let me see if I can find her with our group app," Olive said.

"I'll get my wallet and keys so I can drive you wherever you need to go," he offered.

"You don't have to. I can get an Uber."

"I do have to. I wasn't kidding when I said I like you, Olive. I'm not going to just send you off to deal with this on your own."

She looked at him with wide, solemn brown eyes and he knew he had to tell her the truth. But not now. "Thank you. Delaney is like a sister to me. I'm really concerned about her. I don't know why she would be arrested. The last time was because she was high and drove her car into the front of the Louis Vuitton store on Michigan Avenue."

He saw how upset and worried she was for her friend. Going to her, he put his arms around her and hugged her close to him. "Whatever this is, we'll figure it out together."

"Together?" she asked.

"If you want me by your side, I'll be there," he said.

She nodded. "This thing you wanted to talk about…can it wait?"

"Yes," he said. It had to. He wouldn't add to the anxiety she had. "Don't worry about it."

Her phone rang. "It's Paisley."

"Talk to her. I'll be right back so we can go right away if we need to," he said.

He left her, hearing her voice as he ran up the stairs to his bedroom and put on his shoes, grabbing his wallet and keys from the dresser.

He caught a glimpse of himself in the mirror again and glared at himself. Here he was playing the hero, being the kind of man he wished he truly was, all the while knowing that what he had to tell her was going to hurt.

Because somehow over the last few weeks he'd changed roles with Olive. Now he was the one who was playing games with the people in his life. Dating her because she looked good on his arm... Was that what he'd done? Or was he sleeping with her because he liked that he was good enough for her now?

And what did that say about him?

Nothing good.

He went back down the stairs and Olive was still on the phone, so he hung back to give her some privacy.

So chivalrous.

God, he hated his smart-ass internal conscience that didn't let him hide in any of the behaviors he hoped that Olive would see as noble.

Olive didn't know how things could change so radically in less than an hour, but they had. She'd gone from the absolute high of feeling like she was in love and maybe, just maybe, she'd done enough to right the scales in her favor. But a part of her had acknowledged that she didn't really think she had done enough to deserve forgiveness. Not yet.

But to be fair, Dante wasn't rushing her out the door. Maybe whatever he had to tell her was something good. It could be, right? she thought hopefully. However, right now she had to set that aside and focus on this thing with Delaney. Paisley wasn't sure what had happened either, when she called her.

"I'm trying to get information. I have our lawyer down at the courthouse, but they haven't set bail for her yet. She was arrested for trespassing on Malcolm's house. I did get that out of the desk sergeant." Paisley blew out a breath. "Also *Wend-Z City* has pictures of her being cuffed and dragged from his house while the douchebag stands there with his arms crossed watching her leave."

"I really hate that bastard. Okay, where is she? Dante and I will go wait for her to be released," Olive told her.

Paisley divulged the name of the precinct Delaney was being held at. It wasn't that far from Dante's place. "Do we know why she was at Malcolm's?"

"I don't. She was fine at work today."

"I thought so too. I read his statement that he'd told her repeatedly that things were over but she didn't seem to get the message, so he had her arrested for her own good. Give me a break! He has never done anything for Delaney's own good."

"Exactly. Oh, crap. Listen, I have to go," Paisley

told her. "The lawyer just texted that Delaney's family is involved. She's not exactly going to love that."

"I'll see if they will let me see her. Text me, okay?" Olive said, picking up her bag and turning to find Dante standing in the hallway, a discreet distance from her, just waiting. She smiled when she saw him there, and he smiled back as she walked toward him. "Bye, Pais." She hung up the call but kept her phone in her hand.

"Where are we going?"

She gave him the address of the precinct. "Not too far, right?"

"Nope," he answered.

"Delaney's family is involved, and I don't know how she's going to feel about that."

"I guessed when they started blasting *dish soap heiress* they would be," Dante mused.

"You're not wrong. She hates being called that. Her dad is really nice and loves her, but when he gets involved, everyone better hold their breath."

"He's a force of nature?"

"Sort of. He has a really keen sense of justice and so, if Delaney is in the wrong, he will make sure she pays for it. But if Malcolm is doing something shady…well, Mr. Alexander will hang him out to dry." Olive realized she'd learned a lot from Delaney's family when she'd been making over herself and her own life. She'd watched the way they'd used their money but didn't let it be how they were defined. It had been eye-opening, and it had taught her to look beyond the superficial.

"Sounds like my kind of man," Dante said.

"He'd like you. He has a lot of respect for people who work hard," she told him.

"So not just wealth?"

"Yeah. It's odd because their family has had money for generations, but each new generation has to earn their way."

"Even Delaney?"

"Yeah, even her. She doesn't like to give off the image of working all the time, but she's really good at her job with us. So she earns it," Olive said. As much as they might joke that Delaney showed up when she wanted to, the woman did work hard and brought in high-paying clients.

Dante led the way to the garage where there were six cars parked. She was impressed that only one of them was an over-the-top Bugatti. The one he'd driven her home in. The other vehicles were an old Range Rover, like from the 1980s, a ragtop Karmann Ghia, a massive pickup truck, an electric car from a start-up, and a station wagon.

"I get most of these…but the *station wagon*?"

He shrugged. "Oh, my best friend and his wife just had a baby, and they will only let me take my goddaughter for a drive in a sensible car, so I bought that as a joke," he said.

"All of your cars except the sports car are sensible," she pointed out.

"I know," he said, stopping to turn and face her. "When Rosie was born, she was early and had to stay in the hospital in a special unit for three weeks. So I did it to make them laugh."

"Did it?"

"Yes," he said.

It fit with what she was coming to know of Dante Russo. He used his wealth not as a shield against other people but to help them. And she knew this was a small thing, but it just made her fall for him a little more. That should worry her because he "needed to talk" to her. But it didn't. It just renewed that hope inside her that maybe she'd done enough to earn this man in her life.

"You're a good man," she said softly.

"Uh—"

"Don't argue. You are. You're still sexy," she reassured him with a wink. Since she knew men objected to good qualities being called out as if it took away from their macho sex appeal. Maybe in movies, but in real life she needed a decent man by her side.

She *wanted* a decent man by her side.

They took his Bugatti to the police station and Dante dropped her off at the entrance, since it was still rainy, before he parked.

She took a deep breath as she walked inside. This

was only the second time she'd been in a police station and she realized she didn't like being there.

She went to the desk and asked if she could see Delaney.

Dante sat in the car, not really sure he wanted to go into the police station and talk to Olive. She had called him a good man when he felt like anything but.

He called Max.

"Hey, D," Mia answered instead of her husband.

"Mia, hey. How's it going?"

"Good. Max is giving Rosie a bath," she said. "We haven't chatted in a while, so I thought I'd pick up."

"You're right, we haven't," he said. He loved Mia like a sister, but he didn't think she'd be very helpful right now.

Maybe it was the universe telling him he didn't need to talk this out again. Hell, he knew he didn't need to. He already knew what he had to do.

"So Olive Hayes…" Mia said.

"Max told you. I'm not surprised. Yeah. She's really different than she used to be," he said.

"I know. I didn't say anything to you because she's in your past, but she came to our sorority meetup a few years ago and apologized to everyone who was there. We had a nice chat. She seems like she had a wake-up call," Mia murmured.

"Yeah, I see that too. Actually, the woman she is today is very different from who she was in college."

Mia laughed. "You're not wrong. So what are you calling for?"

"I need to talk to Max."

"Oh, man stuff?"

"No, it's about Olive. Did Max tell you she didn't recognize me?"

"Yesss. And that you thought about sleeping with her and then breaking up with her. To which I said, when did Dante get so dumb."

He fake laughed. "Why dumb?"

"You are never going to be impersonal about Olive. There's no way you'd sleep with her just to hurt her, that's not you, and if you did sleep with her... OMG, you did, didn't you?" Mia asked.

"Yeah. Max didn't tell you?"

"No. But to be honest, we've been really busy. He did tell me about your job offer, which I told him to go for," Mia said. "He's been...odd lately. He said it's just the job, but I think fatherhood isn't what he expected and...other things."

Wait a minute. Was his friends' marriage in trouble? How had he allowed himself to become so self-obsessed that he'd missed that? "I don't think so. It's the job. He told me he hates it but didn't want to add to your burdens."

"He did?"

"Yes. You know what...why don't I babysit Rosie this weekend and you two take my place at the lake for the weekend? Just the two of you. You can leave

Saturday morning. I have the Brewers Association dinner on Friday."

"I don't know. I mean, we've never left Mia with—"

"Anyone but me. Because I'm her godfather and a good babysitter. You said so yourself."

"You had your mom come and stay with you," Mia pointed out.

"Yeah, but I learned a lot from her. Let me do this for you two," Dante said.

"Okay. Max is done. I'll pass him the phone."

He heard her handing it over.

"Hey, D. What's up?"

They both always asked him that. He knew they always had his back, but he wondered if he'd leaned too heavily on them. "I'm good. Just was calling to see if you'd talked to Mia about the job and she told me you had."

"Yeah. Thanks again. I'm going to go for it."

"I'm glad. I set everything in motion with HR. Also, I offered Mia the cabin this weekend so you two can get away."

"Uh, what?"

"Yeah. You both need some couple time," he said. "Don't ask me how I know."

"Thanks, D."

"It's nothing. You'd do the same for me," Dante said. "I've got to go. Talk tomorrow?"

"Yeah. Thanks again. Love ya, man."

"Love ya too."

He hung up and got out of the car. He'd been so busy trying to figure out if Olive was using him at first, then if he could use her, he'd let himself forget the man he'd always been. He was going to tell Olive the truth and then he was going to apologize and figure out how to keep her in his life because, if he'd figured out one thing when he'd been talking to Mia, it was that he wanted what Max and Mia had.

He wanted it with Olive, and he was pretty sure they could be happy together. He just had to move on from the past once and for all. The way that Olive already had.

He pocketed his keys as he walked up to the door of the police station, his head bent against the wind. He heard someone behind him and noticed it was a woman, so he held the door for her.

"Thanks."

She rushed to the desk and he looked around, finally spotting Olive sitting on one of the benches to the side. He hurried over to her and sat down next to her. "Did you find out anything?"

"Just that I can't see her yet. She's not allowed visitors. We are waiting to find out if bail has been set."

"So, we just wait."

"Yeah," she said. "I hate this."

"Me too," he said. "Hey, do you have any plans this weekend?"

"Just the brewers' dinner with you," she said.

"I like the sound of that," he murmured. "I'm babysitting my goddaughter for the weekend. Want to help me out?"

Her mouth dropped open. "You *babysit*?"

"Why does every woman doubt I can do this?" he grumbled. "Actually, my mom came and helped out last time, but she got me sorted."

Olive laughed and nodded. "Yes, I'd like that. Unless Delaney needs me."

"Fair enough."

"Olive. Glad you're here," another woman said.

He turned to see it was Paisley Campbell; she'd been in several of his classes in college. They'd both been business majors. Would she recognize him? Please, God, don't let her. He wanted to be the one to tell Olive who he was.

"Paisley, this is Dante Russo. You didn't get to really meet him that night when he gave me a ride home."

He stood up and held his hand out to her. "Nice to meet—"

"Danny? Hey, you've changed a lot since college."

Fuck. His heart sank as he glanced around at Olive, wondering if she'd make the connection, and one look at her face told him she had.

# Thirteen

Olive was trying to figure out how Paisley knew Dante, but that didn't make sense. Still, something on his face was almost unreadable and there was a sinking feeling in her gut that told her the answer. But she ignored it. "How is this possible?"

"I went to Northwestern," he said, but before he could say anything else, there was a commotion at the door as H. Baxter Alexander—Delaney's dad—came in, followed by a passel of paparazzi. He walked straight to the police desk where both she and Paisley had been told to wait, and leaned down to speak to the officer on duty.

The paparazzi snapped photos until the duty officer told them to wait outside. It was a distraction for Olive from Dante, or rather, *Danny*. Had their paths crossed in college? She just didn't know, but if he'd had classes with Paisley, there was a pretty good chance he'd been in her inner circle.

She was attempting to process that bit of news while smiling and trying to act like nothing had changed, but she was spinning out of control.

"Hello, ladies," Delaney's dad said, coming over to them. "I'm sorry for sending the lawyer you had hired away, but this needed my attention. Malcolm has been making threats privately to me and I'm not surprised that Delaney went to confront him. But this ends now. I am going to give a statement to the press when she's released... Could you both try to get her ready?"

"Yes, sir," Olive replied. "But they won't let us see her."

"They will now," he said. "I spoke to the judge myself and she will be released shortly."

He noticed Dante and turned to hold his hand out to him. "H. Baxter Alexander."

"Dante Russo."

"Russo... Inferno Brewing?"

"Yes, sir," Dante said.

"I've been watching your company since it came on the scene," he said, then abruptly turned as they heard the door open behind them.

There was Delaney, looking worse for wear. Her

mascara had smudged and somehow she only had one shoe on. And, holy moly…her sundress had mud stains on the hem and was torn. She looked at her father and he looked back at her for several tense moments.

Then he walked over to her and gave her a hug. They spoke quietly and Olive turned to Dante.

"I was the girl who was mean to you?" She knew it deep down but needed to hear him say it. Why hadn't he mentioned this at the beginning? If he knew her, how could he keep this from her?

There was no chance that she was hearing warning bells for the wrong reason. This was karmic balancing on a universal level, and maybe later she could process that and have it make sense. But right now, she was breaking. The mean girl in her wasn't anywhere to be found and what was left was just Olive. Vulnerable and hurt and alone. It had been a long, emotional day and one of her best friends was in jail. And now *this*.

"Yes," he said. His voice sounded huskier than normal and in his eyes she saw the same hurt she felt. But right now she couldn't deal with this. She felt like she was going to shatter into a million pieces.

"Why didn't you say anything to me?" she choked out. What would she have done if he had?

"I didn't think it would matter at first," he admitted gruffly.

"But then you knew it would," she said. "Once

we slept together, or when I told you how horrible I was…why didn't you—"

"I tried—you were so vulnerable."

She had been vulnerable to him because she'd been falling for him. "Did you do this to hurt me?"

"No. Not that."

"Then what?" she whispered.

"I… I'm sorry I didn't say anything sooner."

"I can't deal with this right now," she said. She looked over at her friends, and Delaney looked shattered. As shattered as Olive herself felt. "I have to help Delaney," she told him. She could tell by the look on his face he wanted to reach out to her, ask her to stay, but he didn't.

She took a deep breath and walked over to Delaney and Paisley. Both of her friends looked like she felt. Worn out. Life sure wasn't loving them right now. Delaney's dad left to clear up the paperwork and they were shown to a private office where Delaney got changed into the outfit her father had brought.

"What happened?"

"Malcolm is up to no good. He's doing some shady business and he tried to blackmail my dad with the threat of leaking some photos of me. Dad called his bluff, which is fine, I've had nudes leaked before. But I couldn't just let him win. I know he had some information in the safe at the house, and since it was his weekend with Stanley and I'd dropped him off at the corporate airport, I figured that Malcolm wasn't home…"

"So you tried breaking in," Olive said, taking the small hair straightener out of her bag and plugging it in so she could do Delaney's hair.

"Yes. But he's changed staff and the security code to his place…so I had to climb over the security fence and I triggered a silent alarm."

"Did you get whatever it was?" Paisley asked.

"I don't know. I did open the safe…fortunately, he didn't change that code," she said. "I took a bunch of photos of everything in there but didn't have time to check it out before the cops and the security people arrived."

"I'm glad you got it," Olive said as she stood behind her friend and did her hair. She felt like she was numb to everything, and concentrating on Delaney was helping her to not be overwhelmed by the gnawing hole in her heart.

"Me too. I'm still mad, and now everyone thinks I just can't let Malcolm go. As if! When it's over, it's over, am I right?"

Paisley made a murmuring sound and Olive didn't say anything. She was trying to deal with the fact that Dante had known her in college. Well, not Dante… Danny. She wasn't sure she remembered him now, but did that even matter? Yes, it did, she realized. It mattered on so many different levels and she wasn't sure how she was going to move past it.

Maybe she wasn't meant to.

Maybe this was just one more sting of karmic justice. A sign that it was too soon for her to try to find happiness. She was still paying for her past.

She sighed but it came out ragged, and she realized she was on the edge of tears. She wasn't going to break down here. She needed to be strong for Delaney.

"You okay?" Delaney asked.

"No. But I can't talk about it, Dellie. Why do you ask that?"

"You've straightened the same strand of my hair five times," Delaney said, taking the hair wand from her. "I've got this. What's up with you?"

"Nothing."

She didn't want to talk about her dating woes while her friend was facing trespassing charges and about to be hounded by the press. Paisley came over and put her arm around the two of them.

"Olive didn't know that Dante is really Danny, who we went to college with," Paisley told Delaney, then turned to her. "I think he asked you to dance at the spring formal and you said no woman who had any self-respect would dance with him. But you still had the mic on—"

*Oh, God.* Oh, no. That night… She remembered him now. Danny. That smart, geeky guy she'd brought coffee to and who had helped write her part of the psych paper. The guy who'd always waved at her when she was walking around on campus. The guy she'd made fun of behind his back. This was horrible.

"Everyone heard it. And he just turned and walked away," Olive said.

He'd had that shaggy hair he'd had when she'd first met him in his office, and those same green eyes and that smile. But he'd been just so not the kind of man she'd seen herself with. She'd done more than reject him, she'd humiliated him in front of everyone.

She wasn't sure what it meant that he hadn't mentioned this to her. Was it just that he hadn't wanted to say anything if she didn't know him? Or was it that he'd seen a chance to get a little payback?

Dante wished he'd said something to Olive sooner, like five minutes sooner. He couldn't blame Paisley or anyone other than himself. The police station was suddenly very busy with the higher-ups in the city all streaming in and talking to Delaney's dad. The man had a commanding presence and though he had more money than God, he was gracious and respectful of the police. He knew they had a tough job to do and he never made excuses for Delaney who, if rumor could be believed, had had a few run-ins with the law before.

But he knew that gossip could be dangerous to listen to. Dante scrubbed a hand over his jaw. He had no idea what to do. His gut said to find Olive and explain everything, but she was in crisis mode and helping her friend. And he didn't want to make things worse for her. He didn't want to add to her burden.

This situation with Delaney was the type that had made IDG into the powerhouse company it was. They were experts at taking bad press and spinning it. He knew he needed to give Olive space to help Delaney. He toyed with leaving, but he knew that he wouldn't. If Olive asked him to, of course he would, but he couldn't just disappear until he'd talked to her again.

Dante had known better than to lie. Had known better than to keep this secret for as long as he had. Why hadn't he just come clean? In the deepest part of his soul, he knew the truth. And he didn't hide from it now. He hadn't told her because a part of him believed she'd see past the makeover to that chubby, unkempt guy he'd been. Part of him wasn't sure she'd feel the same way toward him if she remembered who he'd been. If he'd just told her at dinner instead of making excuses. He liked Olive…more than *liked* her. He thought he might be falling in love with her. But how could those emotions ever be real if he kept their shared past from her?

He'd known that, but hadn't had the balls to just own it. It was hard for him to admit she'd hurt him as deeply as she had.

People on campus had refused to meet his eye after that humiliating incident and he'd lost that "golden princeling" feeling his mom had imbued him with.

He'd started to take a hard look at himself and change had followed.

It had been a difficult period but he'd gotten through it and had thought he'd grown into a different man. Until Olive Hayes had walked back into his life. And this time he'd had the power. He had to give himself low marks for the way he'd handled that.

The door where Olive had disappeared opened, and Delaney sauntered out, looking proud and regal, like she was walking the red carpet at the Met Gala. He noticed she was wearing both shoes now. Behind her were Paisley and Olive. Olive's eyes met his and then skittered away.

He stayed where he was, giving them space. The police department had a pressroom, and they moved Mr. Alexander and Delaney into there. Paisley and Olive followed them. Dante tagged along. Catching up to Olive, he caught her arm.

"What?" she asked, her tone the one he remembered from so long ago.

He dropped his hand from her arm.

"I'm stressed and I just don't know what to think. I mean, Dante...how could you—"

"I'm sorry, Olive. More than you could possibly know," he rasped. "I wish you'd heard about it from me. But I didn't know how to tell you..."

"I wish I'd heard it from you too," she said, her voice dipping a bit as she wrinkled her nose and looked away from him, trying to compose herself.

"I... Should I wait for you to finish? I can sit out there and just wait," he said. "Or I can leave. But I think we need to talk."

"I don't know."

"Olive, I wasn't lying earlier. You are important to me. I don't want to leave you while you are like this—hurt by something I did. I just want a chance to discuss this."

"Can I text you later?" she asked quietly.

"Yes. That's good."

She nodded and went to the front of the room with her friends, watching as the press and paparazzi were let in. Delaney smiled at them and joked as they took their seats; it was hard not to buy into the fact that she was in control now. But he remembered how she'd looked when she'd first come into that room. She'd been broken and small.

He listened to the press conference and Delaney deliver the message that she'd gone back into her ex's house for an heirloom bracelet she'd left behind. It had belonged to the first dish soap heiress, Emmeline Lucinda Alexander. She talked about how she'd needed to have it for an event.

Dante's gaze drifted from Delaney to Olive, who stood behind her friend.

Earlier this evening, he'd stood by her side and dreamed of their future, and now all of that was up in the air. His gut was telling him she'd changed. That the woman he'd come to know was who she *truly* was. But this story they'd concocted for Delaney felt a little too pat, and he realized how good these women were at creating an image. Could he trust the one he thought he knew of Olive?

Part of him believed if he played this right, if he was humble and kind, he might be able to navigate his way through this, but another part of him wasn't so sure.

He'd done a good job of forgetting that night until now. It had been a wake-up call, or maybe a baptism by fire. Everything in the world had changed in that one moment as he'd shoved down the unease of going up to ask her to dance, only to have her not just say no but to reject everything that he was.

Sure, she looked small and vulnerable now, but he knew that underneath that shell was a woman who wouldn't hesitate to cut him to the quick. She'd almost done it in the hallway when they'd been coming to this room.

He wanted to find the real woman. Was it the one he'd known over the last month or was it the girl he'd met in college? Or was she somehow something more complex and maybe a little bit of both?

Dante knew he was something more than the tubby nerd he'd been and the billionaire bachelor he was now. But it was harder than he'd expected it to be to just forgive and keep his guard up at the same time. Because as much as he wanted to believe that Olive wasn't really the Olive Hayes she'd been in college anymore, he also didn't want to have fallen for a woman who wasn't who he thought she was. He didn't want to be vulnerable and have been played again.

Olive wasn't exactly sure what they were going to say to each other, but after the press conference she'd texted him and now, two hours later, they were sitting together in a bar. He'd originally offered her a ride home, but she'd realized she wanted this settled tonight. She wanted to wake up tomorrow and have this far behind her.

They had their drinks and were seated in a banquette at the back of the bar. It was dark and quiet as it was a weeknight.

"So…should I go first?" he asked.

She nodded. "You're the one who was keeping the secret. Why were you?"

He rolled his neck, as if trying to relieve the tension, and she realized this wasn't any easier for him than it had been for her. She had felt a bit like the victim before, but she was beginning to see there was no winner in this situation.

"Obviously, I didn't know who Kiki was hiring and when you walked into my office that first day… well, I didn't know what to expect. Do you remember when we met back in college?"

"Yes. I do. I didn't at first, but now it's all come back to me." She swallowed hard. "And I am sorry for how I treated you back then," she said. "But this isn't about that."

"Seriously? This is *all* about that," he snapped, then shook his head. "The thing is, Olive, you weren't what I expected, and I figured I'd just keep the work thing going. You knew your stuff and had good ideas."

"Thank you. I think the business idea was a good one for us. Too bad we had mad chemistry."

He exhaled roughly. "I know, right? So then things began to happen between us, and you told me about your past, and I realized that I was one of the faceless people you'd encountered. I just didn't know how to tell you it was me, and when you apologized for the girl who'd hurt me…well, I accepted it on behalf of the faceless men."

She nodded, her heart heavy. She had the feeling that her karmic ledger was still too marked with red. And this was the long-term fallout of her long-ago deeds. Her therapist had said she had to forgive herself and the hurt she'd caused, but Olive knew that she'd hurt herself too. She was never going to truly have a chance with Dante. He was pretty much telling her he wasn't sure if she'd changed. He'd accepted her apology for the faceless men, but what about him?

How could she prove that? And could she forgive him for lying to her? She understood that he hadn't wanted to bring it up, but he'd had to know sooner or later it was going to come up.

"I appreciated it." It did mean more to her than he'd know. He was right when he'd said he had been a faceless boy. She really hadn't seen him back then.

"Me too. Then you kissed me and wow…so I wasn't exactly thinking about the past," he admitted.

"Was that why you didn't text me when we got back from Milwaukee?" she asked.

"Yes and no. I wasn't sure if you wanted to return to our 'just business' relationship and didn't want you to feel pressured," he explained. "And deep down I knew I had to somehow tell you about your part in my life."

Dante looked away from her for a minute and then took a long swallow of his drink before reaching across the table and taking her hands in his. "I tried to tell you tonight."

She turned her hands over in his. "I know you did. I wish I'd let you. I just was… I saw this guy who was everything I'd ever wanted but never really known to ask for, and I didn't want anything to mess it up."

"Me either," he said. "But that brings up an interesting point…do you like me because I'm this guy?"

She looked at him, not sure what he was asking. "What guy?"

"The one with the haircut and the clothes you picked out?"

"You looked like this before. I saw that article

they did on you when you made your first million," she said.

"Yeah, I did, but I was an asshole and that's when I decided to go back to being me."

"You? This is *still* you, Dante. You can use this as a reason why you think I like you, but the truth is this is who you are," Olive told him, realizing he had the dual personalities she had. But, really, they were different sides of the same person. "You and I aren't that dissimilar."

"I didn't humiliate you," he said defensively.

"You did. You lied to me and made me believe one thing when the truth was…well, it was harder to hear, but I should have heard it from you. Not Paisley."

She knew despite what he'd said earlier he hadn't forgiven her and maybe he never would. That hurt way more than she'd expected it to. She also wasn't sure she could forgive him.

"I've already said I'm sorry about what I did to you in the past," she reminded him.

"Yes, you have."

"Is it not enough?" she asked.

"I don't know," he admitted quietly. "Full disclosure—I did think about doing something similar to you."

"Full disclosure, you sort of did," she reminded him. She supposed he would be justified in his eyes to do that, which just made her heart hurt that much more. It made sense. She remembered that sorority alum lunch she'd gone to and what a long day that had been. She'd hurt so many people with her little comments and attitude.

"What was your plan exactly?" she asked. Though part of her really didn't want to know.

"I thought about making you fall for me and then dumping you," he said.

"That's a dick move and something I thought was below you. I mean, I get it," she said, standing and moving away from the table. "It would be perfect justice and, in all fairness, you did it. I was falling for you. I bought it all—the sexy guy with a heart of gold, the caring CEO who really was invested in his employees. All of it. You win."

She started to leave but he called her name, and she stopped and turned back to him.

"I don't want to win. I could never have done that to you, Olive. I like the woman you are and respect you too much for that."

She had the feeling in that moment that she'd really screwed herself over all those years ago because she knew that Dante was the man she wanted to spend the rest of her life with. But he could never really forget how she'd humiliated him and how that had made him lie to her. She'd never really be able to forgive either of them for their actions.

"Goodbye, Dante."

"Olive—"

She heard the pain in his voice but she couldn't

do this any longer. Rehashing everything was going to lead them straight back here. And there was no future where they were.

"I'm glad we finally had a chance to talk about the past," Olive managed to say, using the words her therapist had given her. "I will always wish that when we'd first met, I'd been kinder. Given everything that's happened between us, I don't think it would be wise to continue to work together. So, this will be goodbye."

She didn't wait to see if he had anything else to say, just left the bar and, since they were close to her office, walked to her car and kept it together until she got home. Once she was in her house, she let her guard down and cried.

# Fourteen

A million times Dante wished he'd gotten up and followed Olive out of the bar that night, but he hadn't. July had bled into August and he'd tried to come up with a clever way to run into her, but there wasn't one. There was no way to just bump into her even when he'd deliberately tried putting himself in her path. Nothing had come of it.

He'd done it more than once. Unquestionably, the easiest course of action would be to text her, but how was he going to word that text? No matter how many times he'd tried, he couldn't figure out how to say what he needed to. And he knew he had to figure this out. His personal life was affecting his work life.

Kiki was ticked that he'd let his hair grow out again, and he had unkempt stubble on his jaw because in the heat of summer he couldn't tolerate the full beard.

The doorbell pealed and he grimaced that he'd let his housekeeper go home early today. He was definitely not in the mood to talk to anyone.

The doorbell rang again, and he accessed the app that let him see who was there.

Fuck.

It was Max.

He'd been dodging his best friend's personal questions for…well, about the same amount of time since he'd seen Olive. Max had gone through the interview and hiring process and was now officially the legal counsel for Inferno Brewing, which was nice. And work had kept them both busy. But now Max was at his house.

Max turned and walked away from the doorbell camera's range and Dante sat back on his lounger, a bit disappointed that his pal had just walked away like that.

"I can't believe I just had to pick the lock on the side fence to get back here. I need a beer and then we're going to talk."

Dante looked over at Max, who stood on the patio near the pool, glaring at him. "Beer's in the fridge."

"Get me one while I change into my trunks," Max said.

"I'm not your—"

"I drew the fucking short straw, Danny. I'm here because it was me or Kiki, and Mia and I figured you'd let me in without a problem. I just had to pick a lock…something I haven't done since college, and I'm irritated. So don't push it."

Dante stood up, walking over to Max. "Thanks. I'm fine. Get your trunks on and we can drink and shoot the shit."

"We can start there," Max said, going into the house and a few minutes later was back.

Dante knew he had to think of something to say that would pacify his friend. That this was his warning call that he couldn't keep letting the breakup with Olive keep playing such a big part in his life.

Could he even call it a breakup?

They'd slept together twice and had one date. One real date when everything had changed for him. He still wasn't sure how to get her back and even if she wanted to get back with him. He'd lied to her and, no matter how he tried to justify putting off telling her the truth of their past, he knew he'd screwed up.

"Thanks for the beer. Sorry for being an ass. I told Mia this isn't the kind of thing you and I do, but she wouldn't stop nagging me."

"It's cool. Were you an ass to her?" Dante asked. He hoped not; he didn't want to be the reason his friends were fighting.

"Do I look *stupid*? She's the best thing in my life except for Rosie. I'm not going to mess it up," Max said, taking a long swallow of his beer. "We all know it's Olive that is in your head. We're just not sure what happened."

"What do you mean you all know?"

Max gave him an exasperated look. "She's not working with you anymore. You're distracted and not your usual charming self. Even your speech at the Brewers Association dinner was lackluster, and that's not you."

"It was okay," Dante said. "I don't want to talk about this, Max. I don't know how to fix it and you know I always have a plan. I'm just regrouping. I will shave and get a haircut and be back in the office on Monday ready for anything."

"Great. Make sure you are," Max told him. "I wish I had some advice for you, but pretty much when Mia and I fight, I freak. First, I'm pissed. Sometimes at her, usually at me for overreacting, and I know I could just say I'm sorry, but I hate that. It's hard being in a relationship long-term."

"How do you do it? You two always seem to figure it out," Dante murmured.

"I just remind her that she's the best thing to ever happen to me. I don't know if that will work with Olive…but it can't hurt if that's the way you feel."

He *did* feel that way. He wasn't as sure she felt the same way about him. "She found out from her friend about our past. She was conflicted about me not telling her and then I…well, I put it all out on the table. Told the truth about thinking about the revenge thing, and that went over as you might guess."

"Not well, eh? I think honesty was the best in that situation. So then what happened?"

"She just said this had to be goodbye."

"Ouch." Max winced. "How did you respond to that?"

"I didn't. I just let her go," he said.

"*What?* Why?"

"She said goodbye. I'm not going to beg Olive Hayes to give me another chance."

Max put his beer down and sat up, turning to face him. "You're an idiot. She's not Olive Hayes to you anymore. She's just Olive, and you know that. Did you think she'd come back to you?"

"I don't know that thinking played any part in this," he admitted.

"Do you want her back?" Max asked.

Yes. He'd wanted her back since the moment she'd said goodbye. And if his ego hadn't gotten in the way, he would have run after her and asked her to stay.

"Yeah, I mean, if she—"

"No. Don't tell me the safe answers. I will tell you the one thing I've learned being with Mia. Love doesn't have any safety zones. You have to either go all in or you're out."

"Well, hell," he said out loud, but in his mind he was already figuring out how to win Olive back. He

wanted her in his life, and he needed to do everything to show her that the past didn't matter.

Olive's newest client was a challenge. She just
wasn't willing to make any changes to her current attitude, and the message she'd been delivering, which
had come across in her key market as too harsh, was
hard to reframe. The more she talked, the less she felt
the client actually listened, so ultimately this session
felt like a colossal waste of time.

Olive was tired by the time she got back to the office. She slipped her shoes off at her desk and propped
them on the end of it. Then she glanced down at her
phone, hoping for the text that hadn't come.

But to be honest, she wasn't entirely sure what
she would have said had Dante messaged her. She'd
walked away. Had said goodbye and left. That was
it. She'd moved on with her life and, if it was a little
lonely, that was her own fault. All the joy she'd found
with Dante had changed her in immeasurable ways,
and she wished she could find a way to make things
right between them.

She opened her phone, determined to find something to do this weekend instead of just sitting at
home rehashing every moment she'd had with him.

Olive remembered how he'd asked her to babysit with him that weekend…right before everything
had fallen apart. She'd seen a photo of him and his

goddaughter in the society pages and her heart had broken a little more. She loved Dante.

There was no denying it to herself. She'd known it that last time at his house when they'd got caught in the rain. She missed him—desperately. At first she couldn't think of anything but the fact that he'd thought about making her fall for him as revenge. Was he the type of man to hold a grudge? But then she'd realized that he had been telling the truth when he'd said he never could have gone through with it.

"Hey," Paisley said, sticking her head around Olive's office door. "Want some company?"

"Sure."

Olive put her feet down as Stanley trotted in and came over to her to be petted. Paisley and Olive had been dog sitting since Delaney had taken a leave of absence from the business to go to Europe to get away from the negative press around her break-in at Malcolm's house. Fortunately, he had decided not to press charges, so some of the furor had died down around her.

"Still nothing from Dante?"

"No. But maybe I shouldn't be waiting for him to come to me," Olive said. "How could I not have recognized him?"

It was the one thing she'd come back to time and again. How could he have blended into nothingness in her memory but then, as soon as Paisley had mentioned it, everything had rushed back?

"I don't know. You know there is a self-preservation part of our brain that does things to protect us," Paisley said. "I still can't remember parts of my childhood when Dad was running the con."

She gave her friend a sympathetic look. Paisley's father had been a con man who'd sometimes had "respectable" jobs but had turned out to be bilking the elderly out of their retirement. Paisley had found out in college when her father had been arrested. She'd cut ties with him and tried to make amends after he'd died in jail. Olive didn't know all of the sordid details of her upbringing, but it had left Paisley with a disdain for lies. Even white lies. She wouldn't tolerate them.

"Maybe. I just don't know how to get back in touch. I could text him, but what should I say?"

Paisley let her head fall back and stared up at the ceiling and then leaned forward, all excited. "The End of Summer Charity Gala! I happen to know that Inferno Brewing has a table because when I called to book our tickets, they mentioned that we might be at the same table as one or two other smaller groups."

A gala. "Will there be dancing?"

"Yes, of course."

She had an idea, and it just might work, but it was a big gamble. She could do this and humiliate herself and… There was no way that wouldn't clear the ledger, she thought. Also, she knew in her heart of hearts why he'd kept the secret from her. Now she was doing this with the hope that Dante could forgive her. She was doing this with the hope that Dante would give her a second chance. But there was a big risk he might treat her the way she'd treated him.

And even though in the back of her mind that seemed like a chance she didn't want to take, she knew she had to. She needed him back in her life. She needed to prove to herself and to him that the past was truly over. He'd said he'd forgiven her but she still hadn't been able to forgive herself.

This was an opportunity to really let go of it once and for all and to find her way into the future she was only now starting to dream she could have again.

"Thanks, Pais. Once again you have proven why you're the brains of the operation."

Paisley just smiled over at her and raised her eyebrows. "Of course I am."

Dante went back to work and started trying to come up with a plan. He got a message from the head of the End of Summer Charity Gala that they were going to be sharing a table with six people from IDG Brand Imaging. That was good news, because he'd have a chance to see Olive and talk to her.

In person.

That was much better than texting, since he'd be able to see her face and touch her. To convince her that he hadn't been holding a grudge and that he wanted her back in his life.

He glanced through the photos of her on his phone. Well, there were just two. One he'd snapped of the two of them at the concert the night that everything had changed between them.

Dante realized that was when he'd let go of the past, even though he still had wanted to pretend he was hanging on to it. It dawned on him now that he was using that as his escape hatch. As a way to safely leave instead of letting her break his heart.

The other photo was the one where Olive had stooped down to talk to a child in the tent at beer fest, and there was such a sweet smile on her face that his gut clenched. How could he have ever thought that her transformation hadn't been real?

Looking at her face, he could see how open and vulnerable she was. He hadn't wanted to see it before, because if he had admitted to himself that she'd changed, then he would have to admit that he had too.

And while her change had been for the better, it felt like his hadn't been.

He rubbed the back of his neck.

Would she be able to forgive him?

He had no excuse. Everything he'd told himself when he'd been keeping the truth from her now seemed like paper-thin lies. How could he not have seen it? Was he so blind to anything that too closely involved himself that he'd just missed it?

He heard someone at his door and hit the lock

screen so that whoever it was wouldn't be able to see he'd been looking at Olive's picture.

"Hiya, boss. Just wanted to say thanks for inviting me to the End of Summer gala and see if I could bring a date," Kiki said really fast.

"Sure," he said. "I'm going stag, so it's not an issue. Guess you found a non-creeper?"

"I'm not one hundred percent yet, but it seems that way."

"Did you meet him at the bar?" he asked.

"No. Online, playing *Animal Crossing*. He's friends with one of my friends and we hung out and chatted on her island."

Dante hadn't played the video game, but Mia and Kiki and half the staff in their office did, so he was familiar with it. "I'm glad. Can't wait to meet him."

"Yeah, I can't wait for that too. This is our first official date...what's the dress code?"

"Cocktail for women, suit and tie for men," he said.

"I can't wait to see what Ben looks like when he's dressed up. Also, we have been asked if you'd come back on the morning show next week. They want to use you as a local expert on Oktoberfest."

"Sure. Let's plug that we will be holding the monthlong fest here during that segment," Dante said.

"On it. See ya later, boss," Kiki murmured, turning to leave.

After his marketing manager had left, Dante remembered their conversation and realized that Kiki hadn't been afraid to risk her heart again. He'd been letting that long-ago humiliation rule his life for too long. He'd forgotten that before that one moment he'd been a confident and decent guy. He'd let Olive Hayes's words make him into someone he wasn't until he'd finally started to find his way back to his true self.

And then she'd walked in the door.

That had thrown him. He was willing to cut himself some slack for that. But why had it taken him so long to see the truth of who Olive was now?

He groaned as he realized it was because he'd been falling in love with her. The one woman he'd never thought he would allow himself to care about. But it turned out she was the only one for him.

Now he was determined to do whatever it took to win her back. Because he knew, without her, he was always going to feel like he wasn't really living. Wasn't really experiencing all life had to offer, and that wasn't something he was going to tolerate.

A part of him wanted to text her now, but he decided to stick to his original plan. Seeing her face-to-face was the best course of action. And, thankfully, it was only a few days until he would see her.

He got back to work, the idea for a new IPA fresh in his mind. Something that they hadn't done before. A warm, autumn blend that he was going to call Redemption. Everyone who went through the circles of hell needed to find a way out of it.

Especially himself and Olive.

He worked long into the night. When he stepped out into the late August evening, he remembered the last time he'd seen Olive. He was never going to let her just walk away again.

# Fifteen

The venue for the End of Summer Charity Gala was an older warehouse that had been converted into a convention space. The exposed brick walls were in direct contrast to the round tables draped with sumptuous white linen and set for twelve. The theme—the majesty of the summer sky—was reflected in the room, which had large trees draped in white fairy lights between the tables to create the illusion that each table was private.

White summer flowers created the centerpiece on each table, which were also adorned with beautiful candles. Olive stood on the threshold, basking in the sheer majesty of the opulent surroundings, and hoped that it would be a magical night for her. She'd taken care with her appearance, selecting an evening-length haute couture gown that featured a long royal blue skirt with a black band at the waist. The top consisted of two swaths of material, one in white that came up from the side of the waist and covered her left breast before wrapping around her neck and fastening with the black swath that covered her right one. Her back was bare, and she'd paired the dress with elegant strappy sandals.

She had coaxed her shoulder-length bob into an elegant updo that left her neck bare, and wore a pair of diamond-encrusted bow earrings with a drop pearl. She'd taken her time to make sure she looked her best because, well, it gave her an extra boost of confidence and she knew that her heart was counting on her to make everything work tonight.

"Oh, this is gorgeous," Paisley gushed as she came up next to Olive. Jack still wasn't back from visiting his sick grandmother, so they were each other's date for the evening. Paisley was wearing a striking, printed evening dress that was white with bold floral designs interspersed in a random pattern, and her favorite Louboutin heels. The sleeveless dress left her arms bare and the tattoo on her inner left arm visible. It was simple text that read, *A blessed unrest that keeps us moving.*

"It really is. I'm so nervous," she admitted to Paisley. Her friend gave her a one-armed hug and then smiled at her. "You've got this. Remember what Rumi said… 'Love risks everything and asks nothing.'"

She wasn't sure that was helpful but nodded. Then she took a deep breath and realized it was. This was a big risk, but if she didn't take it, she'd always regret what might have been with Dante. He might not be the man she hoped he was. He might be an illusion of her ideal guy because she'd helped make him over. Or he could be everything her gut believed him to be.

That was what she was betting on tonight. Others started to walk in behind them, and she and Paisley went to the table chart and found theirs. They were sharing a table with the staff from Inferno Brewing as Paisley had mentioned, but Olive was surprised to see a woman who had been in her sorority on the list. Mia Richardson. They'd had a long discussion a few years ago and Olive and she had left things on friendly terms.

Why was she at Dante's table?

Then she noticed that beneath Mia's name was Max Richardson. Her husband? Maybe he worked for Inferno Brewing.

"Why are you staring at the names at our table?" Paisley asked.

"Mia is on there. She's one of the women from my sorority that I made some peace with from the past, but I didn't know she knew Dante."

"That's interesting. We all went to the same college, so we're bound to have these crossovers. Why does it bother you?"

"She's one of the women who filed the complaint against me that led to the community service. I know you were graduated by then," Olive disclosed. Paisley was two years older than Olive and had been her big sister when she'd originally pledged her sorority. Between her and Delaney, they'd helped her figure out how to be the better version of herself she was today.

"And you said you two are cool. Just be you. I know it's not really helpful, but remember that Dante is why you are here. Not the past," Paisley reminded her. "You've got this."

"I do," she said, but the confidence she'd had when she'd left her house had waned a little bit. It was one thing to think about doing this at home but something else entirely when she looked around this glitzy ballroom slowly filling with people.

Paisley linked her arm through Olive's and they made their way to the bar, stopping a few times to talk to people they both knew. After they had their drinks, Olive took a big sip of her mojito and a deep breath. In the past, she'd acted without consequences and been surprised when they'd found her. Tonight, she was acting deliberately and knew exactly what she wanted to happen.

If it didn't, life would go on. She knew that. And in her heart, she knew she'd have done everything she could to show Dante how much she'd changed and how much she wanted him in her life.

Paisley was in a conversation with one of her clients and Olive gestured that she was going to find their table. There was a three-piece classical combo playing Vivaldi, and she just sort of drifted through the room to the table. Standing by the name cards, looking for hers. She was moving around the table when she felt someone behind her and turned to look up into Dante's eyes.

"I think you're next to me," he said huskily.

"Am I?" she asked.

She couldn't tear her eyes away from him. Drinking in the angles of his face, the sharp jaw, his dark curly hair, artfully styled. The way his navy suit brought out the green in his eyes. Her heart ached and her stomach was full of butterflies. She was almost afraid to breathe and break this moment.

Dante had ordered a car for the evening. Hoping that he'd run into Olive tonight and maybe make a new start with her. That was a big ask given that he'd let her walk away. But he wasn't counting on it. His mom was a big believer in preparing for a desired outcome, which she'd passed on to him. And he took it to heart.

Max and Mia were waiting at the entrance when he arrived. He was happy to see his friends acting more like their old selves tonight. The tension he'd sensed between them seemed to be gone now.

"Wow, someone dressed to impress," Mia teased him.

"It is a gala," he reminded her. He had gone back to Pietro and had his hair styled again, and then texted Sam to get her advice on his outfit before he'd left his place. He wanted to make sure he was every part of the man that Olive liked. He wasn't pretending to be someone else, just being the best version of himself, and he hoped that would be enough to convince her that he was over the past.

"Which is why I'm wearing a tux, not that anyone noticed," Max grumbled.

"You look great," Mia said, kissing his cheek. "Should Max and I go get drinks while you find our seats? We are at Table Three. Make sure we are all sitting next to each other."

"I'm on it," he said. At the Brewers Association dinner, he'd been seated next to Jeff from Brewing Energy Worldwide and the man had been incredibly boring. The night hadn't been fun. But Dante admitted that was because he'd been missing Olive but too stubborn to admit it.

The event planners had gone all in on the theme of summer skies and the room felt almost like they were outside. The lights that they'd put in those trees woven throughout the room were nice. The table plan was probably listed somewhere, but Dante wasn't about to fight the crowd to get close to it since he knew their number.

He spotted Paisley but she didn't see him. That was probably a good thing, he thought. He kept moving and then stopped as he saw Olive. Her back was to him and he couldn't breathe from how beautiful she was. She turned and he saw her profile and his heart started beating too fast.

God, he'd missed her.

This physical reaction was the easiest to focus on. That combustible chemistry had been between them from the first moment she'd stepped into his office. But he knew the reason why it felt so intense now was that he loved her.

He saw her standing there and he wanted to say the right things, but it turned out that the words weren't there. He didn't want to fuck this up again.

He wouldn't.

He was Dante Russo. Tough guy, sexy-voiced CEO who most of Chicagoland loved.

"What are you waiting for?"

He glanced to his left and saw Kiki standing beside him. She was wearing a cocktail dress, and her pale blond hair had been tipped with the same shade of blue to match her dress.

"What?"

"You stopped walking...oh, it's Olive. No worries... I'll keep everyone from our table," she said. "Give you two some privacy."

"Thanks."

He left Kiki and wove his way through the people who were starting to try to find their way to their tables.

Olive was moving slowly around the table, looking at the name cards. He noticed hers and subtly moved his next to it. Then he stepped up behind her. She smelled better than he remembered and suddenly he was afraid he wasn't going to be able to keep his composure.

He hadn't felt this way. Ever. She was more than he remembered and he ached for her.

"I think you're next to me," he said. Oh, yeah, he was suave with the ladies. *Just be cool.*

"Am I?" she asked, turning to face him.

"Yes. Good thing the last event I attended was dead boring. Remember the Art Institute?" he asked. He was going to keep talking until he figured out how to say the things in his head.

*I missed you.*

*I want you.*

*I'm sorry.*

She nodded but didn't say anything.

"So…um, how have you been?"

She tipped her head to the side, licked her lips and then took a deep breath. "Not great. How about you?"

Honesty.

She always delivered it in spades.

"Same. I was starting to slide back into my lumberjack chic," he admitted.

"It wasn't a bad look for you," she said, but he felt disappointed by her response and had a feeling that maybe he was playing it a little too cool, realizing that wanting to take a chance on his love for her and actually doing it were two very different things.

"Olive—"

"Dante—"

"Ladies first," he said.

She shook her head a bunch of times. "I don't know how to do this. How to see if you want to find a way past all of this. I mean…was goodbye what you wanted?"

"No. I didn't want goodbye."

"Okay. What *do* you want?" she asked hesitantly.

"For this to be easier," he rasped, reaching up to shove his hand through his hair but stopping himself before he did it. He reached out and took her hand in his. "I'm just going to lay this out. I need you in my life, Olive. I want you with me. I love you."

She looked up at him, her eyes wide, but she said nothing, and he realized that he might have left this too late. Maybe goodbye had been enough for her. Should he have waited?

But he couldn't.

Every time he hesitated with Olive, it backfired. If she didn't feel the same way and this was over, at least he'd know.

* * *

Olive took Dante's hand in hers as more people were arriving at their table. She pushed her way past Paisley, who squeezed her shoulder, and she led him outside where the wooden deck that overlooked Lake Michigan was illuminated by large seemingly floating circles of lights. She kept walking until they were the only two people in the area.

Then she stopped.

He'd said he loved her.

Her heart was beating so fast that it was like a drum corps in her head. She closed her eyes.

*Dante loved her.*

He hadn't even heard anything she had to say and he'd told her he loved her.

"Are you okay?" he asked softly. "I shouldn't have just blurted that out."

"I'm glad you did," she admitted. "I'm not sure that I'm worthy of your love, Dante. But I'm so happy you love me. I kept trying to make you into the bad guy in my mind, but the truth is I was the one who set up—"

"Stop." He put a finger to her lips for a brief instant before pulling his hand back. "You already apologized for that. After that moment, nothing is your fault. You were everything that I could have hoped for in a woman and I betrayed you by letting my old fears and my ego get in the way."

"You did?"

"Yes. I was afraid to just accept that you could be

with me and didn't want to tell you about that night because you might see me as that guy who wasn't good enough—"

"You were never *not* enough for me," she said emphatically. "I love you, Dante. I came here tonight because I wasn't sure after I walked away that you'd want me to walk back into your life."

"I've been a complete ass to everyone since I let you walk away like that," he admitted hoarsely.

She smiled at the way he said it and because she knew Dante. He might not have been his usual charming self, but there was no way he'd take his temper out on the people around him. It reminded her of something else. He never said anything he didn't mean.

He really loved her.

"I'm not perfect. I am trying every day to be better, but sometimes I falter," she said. She had to be honest with him. She didn't want him to think that she'd turned over a new page and everything was always great.

"You're just right to me. I'm not ideal either. I think we all falter," he murmured.

Then he leaned down, pulling her into his arms, and she felt the warmth of his breath against her cheek as he whispered, "I love you so much, Olive. I was afraid you were going to cut me out of your life, and I wouldn't have blamed you."

She put her hands on his face, staring into his

eyes. "I was afraid of the same thing. But staying away and not taking action, that's not my way."

"It's not mine either," he said.

He kissed her then. Long and deep, and she wrapped herself around him, holding on to him as if she'd never let him go.

Several minutes later, they rejoined the party and spent the evening laughing and dancing with their friends and bidding on items for the charity.

Mia was sweet and it was nice having a chance to get to know her during the night. A deejay took the stage at the end of the dinner. They all danced, and Olive realized she finally had a chance to remedy that painful memory between her and Dante.

A golden opportunity to right a past wrong.

She pulled Mia and Paisley aside.

"I think I should ask Dante to dance…you know, like he did me all those years ago," she told them.

"You don't have to do that," Paisley said.

"She's right, but if you do… I think it would be special," Mia murmured encouragingly.

Decision made, Olive asked the deejay to play "What Makes You Beautiful" by One Direction and if she could use the microphone before he did. She was so nervous, her palms were sweating, but then she looked down to where Dante and Max were singing along to The Lumineers' song "Ho Hey," and she felt her heart melt. How could she ever have *not* seen the man he was? But now she'd finally found a way to make up for how she'd treated him.

"I'm not sure. This isn't that kind of event…" the deejay said.

"It's really important. I'm not going to be rude or say anything other than that I love my man."

He wasn't immediately down but when Mia and Paisley both joined her on the stage and seconded her request, he agreed.

"We have a request for this next song and a personal note. So, here's Olive," he said, handing her the microphone.

"A long time ago, a man asked me to dance and I told him that no one would want to dance with him and that I certainly wouldn't even if we were the last two people on the planet. Dante, I'm sorry I ever said that, and I wondered if you'd dance with me to this song that in many ways truly sums up how I feel about you."

Dante stepped toward the raised stage and yelled, *"Hell, yes!"*

He opened his arms and she jumped down into them and the deejay started playing the song as they kissed. While their friends clapped and cheered them on, Olive realized that the last vestiges of the woman she'd been were drifting away.

They danced together, singing the lyrics at the top of their lungs, and she smiled over at Paisley, who made a heart shape with her fingers.

They drank too much champagne and danced and sang the night away. Then, when it was time to go home, the two of them went back to Dante's house.

He kissed her slowly and passionately in the foyer before scooping her into his arms and carrying her up the staircase to the master bedroom, where he made love to her. Afterward, they cuddled in one another's arms, watching the moon drifting lazily across the sky and talking about plans for the future.

Both of them sort of rusty and unsure at first but then with more confidence. They fell asleep close to dawn, wrapped around each other. Olive felt like her karmic ledger was finally marked Paid in Full and couldn't wait to embark on her future with Dante.

* * * * *

*Look for the next two books in*
*The Image Project trilogy!*

The Billionaire Plan
Billionaire Fake Out

### #2917 RANCHER AFTER MIDNIGHT
*Texas Cattleman's Club: Ranchers and Rivals*
by Karen Booth

Rancher Heath Thurston built his entire life around vengeance. But Ruby Bennett's tender heart and passionate kisses are more than a match for his steely armor. Anything can happen on New Year's...even a hardened man's chance at redemption!

### #2918 HOW TO CATCH A COWBOY
*Hartmann Heirs* • by Katie Frey

Rodeo rider Jackson Hartmann wants to make a name for himself without Hartmann connections. Team masseuse Hannah Bean has family secrets of her own. Working together on the rodeo circuit might mean using *all* his seductive cowboy wiles to win her over...

### #2919 ONE NIGHT ONLY
*Hana Trio* • by Jayci Lee

Thanks to violinist Megan Han's one-night fling with her father's new CFO, Daniel Pak, she's pregnant! No one can know the truth—especially not her matchmaking dad, who would demand marriage. If only her commitment-phobic, not-so-ex lover would open his heart...

### #2920 THE TROUBLE WITH LOVE AND HATE
*Sweet Tea and Scandal* • by Cat Schield

Teagan Burns will do anything to create her women's shelter, but developer Chase Love stands in the way. When these enemies find themselves on the same side to save a historic Charleston property, sparks fly. But will diverging goals tear them apart?

### #2921 THE BILLIONAIRE PLAN
*The Image Project* • by Katherine Garbera

Delaney Alexander will do anything to bring down her underhanded ex—even team up with his biggest business rival, Nolan Cooper. But soon the hot single-dad billionaire has her thinking more about forever than payback...

### #2922 HER BEST FRIEND'S BROTHER
*Six Gems* • by Yahrah St. John

Travel blogger Wynter Barrington has always crushed on her brother's best friend. Then a chance encounter with Riley Davis leads to a steamy affair. Will the notorious playboy take a chance on love...or add Riley to his list of heartbreaks?

# HARLEQUIN
## PLUS

Announcing a **BRAND-NEW** multimedia subscription service for romance fans like you!

---

## Read, Watch and Play.

Experience the easiest way to get the romance content you crave.

Start your **FREE 7 DAY TRIAL** at
<u>www.harlequinplus.com/freetrial</u>.

that was making it hard for her to breathe. She was so happy to see him and to be there.

That felt ridiculous, if she was honest. And scary. She didn't want to be this happy to see a man...to see Dante. She still wasn't sure if she liked him because of him—

*Stop*, she ordered herself. *Stop looking for reasons not to like this man.* Sometimes it was okay to just take a man at face value.

"It's not. I bought it for my parents but they refused to move into the city," he said.

"Where do they live?"

"Schaumburg," he said. "You said you're from Texas...what part?"

"Dallas area. Southlake. I went to college at Northwestern."

She noticed something cross over his face, but it was gone so quickly she wasn't sure if she'd imagined it.

"I figured dinner here would be more private than a restaurant. I want the chance to talk to you tonight," he said quietly.

"Oh?"

"Well, we kind of changed things up last weekend and I know you said you had no regrets... It's always better to have those kinds of conversations alone," he said. "Can I get you a drink?"

"I wouldn't say no to a glass of wine," she said with a smile. "Sorry if that's sacrilege to you."

"It's not. I was planning to grill us some steaks for dinner and have a couple of wines to go with it."

"A couple?"

"Wasn't sure if you were a red, white or rosé gal. I know it's not proper, but I really like rosé in summer," he said, leading the way down the hall to a large kitchen. It was modern and sunny.

She saw obvious prep work had been done for their meal. "This is a big house for one guy."

"It is," he admitted. "I hope to have a family someday. The wine fridge is there if you want to check out the whites and rosés. If you prefer red—"

"Rosé sounds good. I'll pick out a bottle. Do you need my help with anything else?" she asked, trying not to think about the fact that he wanted a family someday. She was trying not to read too much into that.

"No," he said. "I had my housekeeper make a salad to go with the steak, and I'm going to grill some artichoke hearts when I do the steaks."

"Sounds delicious. Do you cook a lot?"

"No," he replied. "I grill in the summer pretty much all my meals. I can fry an egg and eat a lot of microwave oatmeal. Otherwise, Mrs. Flanders preps dinner for me and I heat it up when I get home."

She poured them both a glass of wine and turned to him. "Why did you say you lived in the suburbs?"

"Sorry about that. I figured you wouldn't trust me to be a good guy and see you safely home otherwise," he said.